OUT OF THE DARKNESS

A Novel

JEANNE FORTUNE

If you or someone you know is dealing with depression, please seek help. And if you or someone you know is having suicidal thoughts, please visit the National Suicide Prevention Lifeline at www.suicidepreventionlifeline.org for resources and to chat with someone.

National Suicide Prevention Lifeline
Dial: 988 or 1-800-273-TALK (8255)
TTY Dial 711 then 1-800-273-8255

If you or someone you know is in an abusive relationship, please seek help now. You can visit the National Domestic Violence Hotline at www.thehotline.org for resources and to chat with someone.

National Domestic Violence Hotline
1-800-799-SAFE (7233)
TTY 1-800-787-3224

Other books by Jeanne Fortune

Mommy, I Need My Wheels

Manman, Mwen Bezwen Wou Mwen Yo (in Haitian Creole)

Suzette and the One-Eyed Cat

Suzette ak Chat Yon Sèl Grenn Je a (Haitian Creole)

TABLE OF CONTENTS

ACKNOWLEDGMENTS

I would like to thank my children for making me a mother, and my husband for always supporting me. I want to thank all my family members and friends who have ever gone out of their way to lend me a hand. I could not have done any of this without you.

Special thanks to Dr. Jameson Mercier, Pauline Harris, Redpenits, Suki Tranqille, Sanyam Jain, Cina Jimenez, Grace Bjarnson, Rafi Soule, Sabrina Fonville, Tanya Butterfield-Spady, Elamae Samuel, Logan Masterworks, and MJ Fièvre for all your support and feedback.

FOREWORD

The immigrant story is not one homogeneous story. Rather, it is a collection of stories and experiences. While many know the feeling of leaving their homeland behind, the experiences and consequences that follow, despite some similarities, vary widely. Migrating to the United States, or any other country for that matter, brings about complicated emotions. All too often, and for many reasons, individuals are left to process these emotions alone. They are often unsuccessful and develop deeper and more complicated emotional and mental health issues.

In particular, the mental health of immigrants is rarely a topic of discussion. The conversation tends to focus more on their legal status rather than any trauma they may be fleeing or experiencing. This story sheds light on some of those challenges and the ways immigrant cultures seek to cope. While the immigrant story varies widely, the experience of battling depression and the shame and stigma that often follow weave a common thread. We don't need to have the same experiences to have the same feelings.

Jameson Mercier, Ph.D., LCSW

CHAPTER 1:

LEAVING HAITI

There were two suitcases at the door—one for me, and the other for my sister, Sheila. We were about to leave our country and travel more than one thousand six hundred miles, alone. My mother would stay behind all by herself. She was about to send her two minor children on a journey full of uncertainties, hoping they would have a better life overseas. Her heart was breaking into pieces, but she wanted to save them. From what? She didn't know.

The date was June 13, 1992. It was a beautiful Saturday; we didn't go to church that morning like we usually did. The sun was bright, and the weather was perfect. I stood in front of my house, staring at the coconut tree next to my neighbor's house and at the breadfruit tree next to it. I stared at my neighbors' houses, thinking of my schoolmates and the friends that I'd made there since birth. I was going to miss listening to "antillaise music." I was going to miss "Pè Thomas;" at the time it was my favorite show on television, and it was going to be on that coming Thursday night. I was going to miss those sweet mangos during the summer months.

I spent the day imagining my life on the island with my mom. I started to remember all the things that happened to me while living there. As I stood on my house's steps, I could see myself playing hopscotch with my friends. We had just finished elementary school and had entered secondary school, which was equivalent to middle school in the United States, but we still played like younger kids, including with dolls.

We would get a piece of charcoal. White chalk would not have done a good job since the ground was made of dirt and rocks. We would get a small piece of rag and place a small bucket or cup of water next to us while we played. As the cloth dried up, we would wet it again. I used to be pretty good at that game.

Other days, we would jump rope. At times, more than one person would be jumping and whoever let the cord hit their feet lost. Even though we were girls, we still played marbles and another game we called circle. Circle was played with a round metal wheel. Most kids used a bicycle wheel. One would use a metal hanger and make a hook at one end. The hook was then wrapped around the circle, and the player would hold the other end of the hanger and walk behind the wheel while it was moving. If the circle fell or the hook came off, it was a loss.

Some days we decided to have church. All the kids in the neighborhood would get together in the courtyard and sing Christian songs. Another fun game we played was bus driver. There were several homes in our yard, and all the homes had the same address. The number was posted at the yard's entrance. The mailman would shout the person's name during deliveries, and neighbors would point him to the correct house. Amazingly, neighbors didn't steal each other's mail. Think of it as a gated community, but all the homes inside had the same address. My grandmother's home had at least ten steps and so sometimes we would pretend like the stairs were a bus. One person would be the driver, so that individual would sit on the first step at the bottom, and all the passengers would sit on the other steps, and they would pay the driver pennies for the ride. We would all make engine sounds with our mouths.

Other nights, we all sat in a circle and cracked jokes. Tim tim? Bwa sèch. The storyteller would ask, "tim tim?" And everyone else would answer "bwa sèch," which means dried wood, but that's not what it meant in that case. It really meant everyone was ready to get started with storytelling. We would take turns telling stories, and other times, one person would ask a question and the others would have to guess the answer.

I thought of the day my dad left us for the United States. I wore a little pink dress that Aunt Claudette had made for me. I don't remember exactly everything that happened that day. Still, I do remember standing between my parents with my siblings right next to me.

I imagined what Dad must have felt inside the plane when it was taking off. I wanted so much to be in there with him. I looked so innocent in those pictures; I thought my dad went to paradise. Right after Dad left, we moved to another house. It wasn't huge, but it was definitely bigger than the one I was born in. It was connected to my grandfather's house. It was a one-room house with a kitchen in the back and concrete floors. My mom bought a bunk bed for my older sister, Sheila, and me, but Sheila never slept in hers; she always wanted to sleep with my mom.

My mom only let me sleep in her bed when I was sick because I used to wet the bed at the time.

"I don't want you to ruin my mattress," she would say when I begged her to let me sleep with her.

Sheila was a cry baby, so she always got to sleep with Mommy. I always thought my mom loved her more than me because she always got special treatment; she was like a princess. She read a book while I cleaned or learned how to cook. My mom saw in her a future; I'm not sure what she saw in me.

"You're a waste of money," she would say to me.

I didn't look down on anyone; everyone was equal in my eyes. She wanted me to have a bourgeois girl's attitude, but I just wanted to be another girl on the block. The bourgeois were considered to be highly educated and wealthy. She sent me to one of the best schools in Haiti, more expensive than Sheila's, so I could have high-class friends and speak French more than Haitian Creole. Still, I preferred to hang out with those who were less privileged than I was, something that many people appreciated about me.

My sister often sat around reading romance books. I, on the other hand, dressed in shorts and flip-flops, walked in the mud of the market to get my mom what she asked me to bring. When I returned from the market, she would give me one gourde, but whenever Sheila asked her for money, she would give her five gourdes. I never understood why Sheila got more than me for doing nothing. I wanted my mom to see that I was responsible and that I could run a house. I wanted her to be proud of me, but instead, she took more pleasure in Sheila and her intellectual development.

"Why don't you send Sheila to the market?" I asked her one day. "Do you love her more?"

She looked at me with pity.

"I only send you because you have good taste and pay less for good products. I love you guys the same."

But her actions didn't match her words. She gave me five gourdes that day to shut me up, a big kiss, and a big hug that put a smile on my face.

Then came the time when Sheila was becoming a woman. She had her first period. I didn't really know what that meant, but I used to see my mom's menstrual cloths hanging outside our house, super white. Back then, it wasn't unusual for women to use white cloths during their menstrual cycle since feminine pads were expensive and not as popular. Sheila was too special to wear the kind of cloths my mom wore; princesses weren't supposed to wash them. It became my duty to buy her pads, and I hated the fact that I was becoming my sister's little servant. I hated the fact that we weren't treated equally. At least not all the time.

"I'm older; if I'd killed Mom during childbirth, you would not have been born," Sheila would say to me when I didn't want to do her favors.

Then came the day I was supposed to go buy her pads two blocks from our house. The last street I had to cross was broader than what I was used to. I couldn't see if any cars were coming because a truck blocked my view on the right side. I remember my mom teaching me how to cross the streets, but that time was different, and I was all alone.

"Look left, then right. If you don't see any cars, cross," she had said.

I looked left; there were no cars, but I couldn't see right because of the truck and people who had gathered all over the sidewalk to sell charcoal. I decided to count to ten and run.

All I could hear was the sound of a car's brakes.

The driver cursed at me for almost causing him an accident. My heart started beating so fast I thought my breath was going to leave me. People gathered around me, asking why my mom had sent me out into the streets alone.

My mom never stopped sending me on errands. I explained to her that Sheila could buy her own stuff.

"But Sheila's older now, she can't be seen carrying that stuff," she said.

She offered me more money, one gourde, equivalent to less than twenty cents in US currency.

Dad's friends visited regularly after he left; some stopped coming a few months later, but one of them visited for years. I was always happy to see him on those Sunday mornings because it meant money. He always gave Sheila and me five gourdes each. That used to be a lot of money back then, five whole gourdes.

My Uncle Richard also visited late at night, sometimes while we were sleeping. My mom said he visited so late to see if another man was sleeping inside our house, to report to Dad. As a kid, I never understood those tactics; I always thought he visited late because that's when he had time. I thought he cared about our welfare, so I didn't understand why it bothered my mom so much.

I didn't understand why so many Haitians wanted to live in America so badly. Growing up, I had always heard America was a place with a lot of money. People joked money grew on trees there, and all you had to do was shake a tree and money would fall out of it. I grew up thinking there was no future in Haiti, and so I too would have to leave in order to see beautiful things and have a better life.

I didn't know some people would do almost anything to get there or stop someone else from going there. I had heard stories of people selling everything they owned and risking their lives to get to America by boat. I had heard stories of sharks eating people alive because the boat sank. I had heard stories where individuals had used voodoo to prevent others from leaving Haiti for wealthy countries. They had the attitude that one must not succeed or get ahead of another. It was a culture where few people wanted to see good things happen to others.

I thought of when I used to go to school, and my mom would give me one gourde for lunch. That's less than one quarter. My cousin Johanne's mom always gave her five or ten gourdes. Johanne and I were the same age, so we attended the same school. I wanted so much to have Johanne's life. She got to eat a sandwich and soda at school, while I only had enough money for chips, roasted peanuts, or fresco, which is crushed ice with flavored syrup. Think of it as a snow cone. Sometimes Johanne shared with me, other times she didn't. I craved what she had, so I complained to my mom.

"Why can't I have a dollar for lunch like Johanne?" I asked.

"Because I can't afford to give you a dollar," she said.

She explained to me that I had to learn to live with what I had. I should be happy with my chips because while I was eating them, another child was going hungry. And so, I stopped complaining and ate my chips or whatever I could afford.

I adored my mom; every day after school, I brought her at least one chip from my bag. If I ate cookies for lunch, I brought her a piece; if I had candy, I did the same. I wanted her to know that I was thinking of her. I remember one day I ate all my lunch. When I got home from school, I ran to her as usual and kissed her on the cheek. Haitian children greet grown-ups with a kiss on the cheek. I could smell rice and beans and a legume (vegetables) dish coming from the kitchen. I then proceeded to go inside to remove my school uniform before she yelled at me to do so.

"Coucou!" she said.

That was her nickname for me, but my real name was Cynthia Josaphat.

"You didn't bring me anything today?"

"No," I replied, "I ate all of it."

I was thinking at that moment I had spoiled my mom. From that day on, I never forgot to bring her something, unless I went to school empty-handed, which did happen sometimes.

I came home from school one day, and she was crying; she didn't want to tell me what was wrong. I wasn't sympathetic, so I went outside to play with my friends, leaving her crying inside the house. For some reason, she trusted Sheila more, maybe because Sheila would wipe her tears and give her a hug while she was crying. She had received a cassette tape from Dad; someone had lied about a man sleeping in our house. So instead of defending herself, she just sat there and cried. A few days later, she had bumps all over her legs; it must've been a reaction to what Dad told her, since she kept it all inside. And so, Sheila told me what

Dad had said on the cassette tape. That was before the internet and cellphones were popular. He accused my mom of cheating with another man and said that he didn't want to be with her anymore. He said that he only stayed with her because of Sheila and me, and that once he takes us away, he'd be done with her. My mom still managed to keep it together; she still had hope that one day Dad would come back for all of us. She still visited his family with us; she even spoke to Uncle Richard, the relative she believed lied about another man sleeping in our house.

Then I thought of the time when we visited Dad's family in Miragoane, another town outside Port-au-Prince. Although I often visited when I was a kid, it was the first time I was going to stay there overnight. I had never been around my grandmother before for an extended time, so I was happy to have been invited. I was treated like a little princess by my grandmother. I was lying down on my stomach one morning when my grandmother came and started rubbing my back. My brother, Paul, stood there staring at her, wishing he were me.

"Don't be jealous," Grandma said to him, "you have me every day. This is her first vacation with me."

I could see in his eyes that he had never gotten a back rub before, although he spent his entire childhood in that house. My brother's mom gave my dad custody of him when he was a small child. Paul never saw her again.

Soon, my cousin, Jacqueline, visited from Paris with her father, who was my dad's brother, Uncle Fritz. Jacqueline and I were the same age. We had just reached our teenage years. The moment she stepped foot inside the house, everything changed. The house had a total of five to six rooms, but Jacqueline slept in the main room in the house, where my grandmother slept. You could call it the master bedroom because it was huge and most of the food was kept in there. Sheila and I slept in one of the other guest rooms. Being able to sleep in my grandmother's room meant someone was special.

Because Jacqueline came from Europe, she also had more money than we did, which meant she could buy food even when there was nothing ready to eat in the house. We spent most of our days sitting on the front porch looking at people walking by and at merchants shouting out the names of their products. Sometimes we would buy baked patties stuffed with ground beef; other times, we would buy boiled corn, and every now and then, we would buy cookies and candy. At night, we would buy fritay (fried meat, fried plantains, fried sweet potatoes, fritters, fried breadfruits) or fried patties with smoked herring from street vendors. Jacqueline would pay most of the time because her dad gave her money.

Jacqueline became the little princess in the house, and I began to receive the same treatment as Paul. Everything revolved around Jacqueline. Sheila and I were barely noticed anymore. Some nights, Jacqueline was allowed in my grandmother's main room while the adults were talking. Sheila, Paul, and I were left in the main house. If we ate in the morning, we didn't eat again until late at night, sometimes after 9 p.m. or the next morning.

We woke up one morning and saw that there was food on the stove; it must've been our lucky day. That morning we were given boiled breadfruit with spaghetti while Jacqueline ate something much more special: boiled sweet plantains with fish sauce. Unlike American spaghetti, where a red marinara sauce is usually served with the pasta, Haitian spaghetti is made differently. The dish is usually made with smoked herring or hotdog with tomato paste and sometimes ketchup which makes it drier than the American version of the dish. I didn't get it. We were all kids; we were all grandchildren, nieces, and nephews. So, why the special treatment for one and not the others?

I was the "bad" kid for not taking anyone's nonsense. It was a big house, a huge one, but I would rather live in my mom's tiny house than feel worthless in a big one. I convinced the other kids not to eat their food, so we climbed a ladder to get on the roof and threw the food on the ground. We were punished—no food for the rest of the day. The way I saw it, I didn't belong in that house. I didn't have to take their nonsense, so I asked to go back to my mom's.

Paul was asked to take me home that same day after I packed my bag and said I would walk back if I had to. Uncle Richard was called to punish us for not eating our food, but I was already home by then. I swore to never step foot in that house again.

The summer Jacqueline visited, my mother found out the United States Citizenship and Immigration Services (USCIS) approved my dad's petition for our green cards. The new school year had just started. By then, I was old enough to do my own hair. A ponytail and a small braid in the front was my favorite hairstyle. I had just finished elementary school and I did not want to be seen with ribbons or ball hair ties. The day we were to take our passport photos, my mom explained to us that my dad would be coming to Haiti in a few months for our visa appointment at the embassy. She made us promise not to tell anyone because she feared others might use voodoo to destroy our chances at a better life outside of Haiti. It was an exciting day. I grew up imagining what it would be like to live in the United

States. I had seen people off so many times. I had seen airplanes get lost inside those clouds. I even thought America was inside those clouds. I had butterflies in my stomach that entire day and for weeks after. My day was finally coming. I was going to see the most beautiful place on earth, or so I thought. The only problem was my mom was not coming with us, but I thought she would soon follow. My dad would never leave her behind because he loved her—or so I thought. I never went back to visit my grandmother, even when I knew I was getting ready to leave Haiti for good.

As the time grew closer to our visa appointment and for my dad to fly into Haiti to take us to the embassy, my mom was busy giving the agency in charge of our files all of our documents. During one visit, the lady in charge informed my mom that my dad had asked her to stop processing our documents because we refused to eat the food his family provided. However, the lady promised my mom she would send everything to the embassy as she was hired to do. While Uncle Fritz told my dad we threw the food away, he failed to tell my dad that his daughter ate something totally different than what had been served to the rest of us that day.

When I was a small child, my dad held my hand to help me write straight with a pencil. I was left-handed, but was forced to use my right hand to write. He took us to the "champs de mars" for ice cream every Sunday and put up with my stubbornness. I remember an incident that happened when I was no more than six or seven years old. We went to the "bicentenaire" for ice cream and watched people roller-skating. I was the laziest kid around; I didn't like to walk. I was there with my dad, my mom,

Sheila, and a lady who worked for us. I stood next to the water fountain with a chocolate ice cream bar in my hand, begging for someone to carry me, but everyone refused.

"You have your own feet too," they said.

They all decided that they were going to pretend like everyone was leaving me, but they would hide somewhere to watch me. Although I was little, I knew they couldn't leave me; I belonged to my parents. So I sat there, enjoying my ice cream and watching people roller-skating. I'm not sure how much time passed, but they all came back laughing, telling me that I was going to be a tough woman. The lady that worked for us finally agreed to carry me on her back because I wouldn't walk.

I thought of the ring my dad sent me with the letter "C" when I was young; I had asked him for it. I thought of the five US dollar bills he used to send me whenever he sent money to my mom for us. I was glad I was going to get to stay with him, but I also wanted my mom to come with us.

I pictured the man the locals stoned to death on my block for stealing what some people said was a pot. His body lay on the street for hours after he was killed. I remembered the man who was burned to death a couple blocks from my house, unable to escape the car tires that were placed around his body, screaming for someone to help him. He was surrounded by a mob screaming "die." A large crowd watched silently. My mother covered my eyes that morning on our way to church. I was probably nine or ten years old at the time. By the time we returned from church, his body had been reduced to a huge piece of charcoal.

My father's name was Michel, but my mom called him Micho. Micho was dark-skinned with a medium built. He was slightly bald with gray hair. His hair changed color when he was in his twenties. He also developed Type 2 diabetes a few years after moving to the United States.

My dad flew to Haiti for our visa appointment. Since my parents were not legally married, my mom was not included in the petition as a spouse. My mom was so excited to hear Micho was coming. It had been nearly seven years since he left. They had not seen each other since. She cleaned the entire house and prepared all his favorite meals. My mom went to the airport that afternoon to welcome Micho home, but she returned alone. I didn't understand.

"Where is my dad?" I asked her.

"He went to Miragoane with Uncle Richard," she replied.

I could see the sadness in her eyes and the embarrassment. She had waited for him all those years. We had all waited for him all those years, and he didn't care to be with us. My dad spent the first two days of his trip in Miragoane with his mother and siblings. He visited us afterward. When I got home from school that day, he was at the house. As hurt as I was that he hadn't prioritized us, I was still happy to see him. I was actually excited to see him. I had grown up with so many friends who did not have fathers either because they didn't care or because they had died, so having my dad with me that day made me feel pretty special. I ran and kissed him. He could not stop touching my hair and my skin, telling me how much I had grown. I was probably getting ready to start second grade when my father had left Haiti for the United States.

My parents finally got married during my dad's trip to Haiti. I wasn't even invited to the ceremony. It was like a joke. She wore a plain white dress that belonged to her sister Claudette, had her hair done like a regular church day, and wore regular white shoes. The reception looked like one of those parties I used to have for my dolls when I was a little girl with soda and cheap cookies.

I thought it was an embarrassment, but she was happy. I'm not sure why she did it, maybe because she wanted to be someone's wife since we come from a society where everyone's expected to act a certain way. Perhaps she wanted to make things better with God since she got re-baptized after Micho left for America, or maybe it was because she loved him. Whatever it was, it was stupid. It was clear to me and everyone else that Micho didn't love her. He didn't even like her. She didn't even get a ring. She wore a cheap ring on her finger for as long as I could remember, and once she got married, she put it on the engagement finger. He didn't give it to her.

During that trip, my father took Sheila, Paul, and me to the embassy for our visa appointment. The consulate officer asked if we were happy to see our father, but all other questions were directed at my dad. At the end of the meeting, the officer asked for his wife. He said he had not added her to the petition. The officer asked my dad to bring my mom the next day. Micho never mentioned it.

Within a few days, my dad left Haiti with Paul. Sheila and I would follow a couple months later. As a bachelor, he had always rented rooms from others, but this time he needed to rent an apartment so Sheila and I could have our own room.

My grandfather got sick a few weeks after the wedding. My sister and I were set to leave in less than two months. My grandfather was in the hospital for about three days, and then the doctors let him come home. Our house was connected to his, but with a different entrance. My grandfather liked me; some say he did because of my light skin, which was closer to his. He wasn't fully Haitian; he was mixed with French, but he could pass for Caucasian. I liked his stories; he always managed to make me pee on myself with his jokes because I laughed so hard.

I remember visiting him the day after he got out of the hospital. He was so skinny, but that was nothing new; he'd always been thin. He became even nicer to me around that time; it was the first time he ever gave me a five-cent coin so I could buy bubble gum. He asked me to visit and comb his hair, which was very soft, straight, and long in the back. I once had to give him a bath because he was too weak to bathe himself. His skin was so dry and ashy. That was the first day I ever saw him step his feet on the ground without socks. He always told me that the earth can attract death, because when we die, we go in the ground. He never let his bare feet touch the ground. He also wanted me to cook him plantain and fish. He didn't like to eat; he preferred soda and cigarettes, but even three plantains were not enough for him that day. He told me stories about myself when I was a child, how he loved my serious character.

Two days later, I visited again, and something was different about him. His eyes had gotten smaller, his cheekbones stuck out, his nose was straighter than usual, and he couldn't eat or drink. In front of my aunt and family, he asked me to brush his hair, and I ran away, afraid that he was going to die and come get me. That night, I heard him moan. He kept me awake the entire night. I prayed that he would either get better or die; I hated the fact that he was suffering. Around four that morning, he placed his watch in my mom's hand and thanked her right before closing his eyes. I went to the funeral, saw tears in everyone's eyes, but I did not shed any. My mom told me at the funeral that she wished Grandpa had died while Micho was in Haiti so she could have support. I didn't understand why she said that because I thought she had Sheila and me.

I had just gotten a relaxer for the first time; my hair was flowing all over my face. I wore a beautiful white dress with red stripes and white shoes.

"Don't embarrass me when you guys get there; make me proud," my mom said.

My mom was so excited that Sheila and I were leaving to go live with my dad; I guess it was a bittersweet feeling since she wasn't coming with us. Her eyes seemed teary and red.

"Micho is a good man," she said. "He will take good care of you guys; I told him that I'm sending you to him in one piece."

It meant we were both virgins.

I was leaving the only home I had ever known, not just four walls with a floor and a ceiling, but a home filled with love. If only I knew what I was getting myself into at the time. I never imagined life without my mom. As far as I was concerned, things were supposed to get better, not worse.

As I got ready for my new life, I remembered those times when I used to get sick, usually with bronchitis. My mom would stay up all night to watch me, rubbing Vicks on my chest, behind my ears, and under my nose so that I could breathe better and cough less. She called me the tough kid, the one she never had to defend.

"I don't worry about you; you can handle yourself," she would say.

I remembered the times when Haiti would be hit with political instability. Those days happened pretty often. My mom would rush to the school to pick us up. She taught us to never take the same route every day.

"You don't want anyone to know your routine," she would say.

But she instructed us to take a specific route during shootings, because that's the route she would take to meet us.

I thought about how my birthday was going to be celebrated in America. I hadn't lived with my dad since I was a little girl. Although he always sent money, I really wasn't used to him. My mom never bought me a cake for my birthday; Aunt Claudette made me one, usually chocolate, my favorite. My mom was not into parties; she wasn't the type of person who would throw a birthday party and invite other kids to come eat. After school on my birthday, she always cooked a big fish, just for me. For me to have a big fish for my birthday meant more than a cake, since I was not crazy about baked sweets.

"Eat your food, and go study," she would say to me afterward. "You will thank me one day when you're something big in life."

I didn't like school in Haiti; the teachers expected me to memorize pages of lessons daily, and it just wasn't my thing.

And so, I thought of the Pathfinders at church, the picnics, the hikes, and the camps I had gone to. I remembered my first camp in Haiti; we went to a town called Grand Goâve. It was the first time I'd ever gone away from home. Although Sheila was there with me, I still missed my bed. I still wet the bed at the time, so I was worried the other kids would make fun of me, but they didn't; a lot of them wet the bed themselves. I remembered the river close to the campground; it was where we took a bath in the morning and in the afternoon. Although I was always afraid of water, I felt pretty comfortable in that river. I could swim under the water and come back up all by myself. When we returned home a week later, I saw the look on my mom's face—it was as if she hadn't seen us in years. I had never seen her so happy in my life. She could not stop hugging and kissing me.

I was going to a brand-new country, and I didn't know if I would find other Haitian children at school. I saw on television that kids got beat up in American schools for no reason. I was thinking of learning English, but I hated to study. How was I going to learn another language? I was happy with my French and Haitian Creole. Overall, I was pleased to be leaving, although I loved living with my mom. I wanted to live with my dad; maybe I would become his favorite child, like Sheila was to my mom.

I sat quietly in the car on the way to the airport; I could not stop imagining what the inside of the airplane was going to look like. I had seen this big bird take off so many times, and I always wondered how those people felt while they were in there. I imagined it to be like paradise, something so beautiful.

"Coucou, we're going to see each other really soon. Your dad will send you guys to see me in five years."

Unlike the airport where I would land in the United States, the airport in Haiti was pretty small, so the airplane stood in the middle of the tarmac. We had to walk out to it. As I walked up the stairs to get on the plane, I knew there was a balcony on one of the upper floors at the airport; family members could go there to see their loved ones take off. I remember walking up the stairs to the plane, but I never looked back. It wasn't that I wasn't going to miss my mom, but I really did want to see inside the airplane. I thought if I didn't get in fast, I might lose my seat. Sheila, on the other hand, stood on the last step, waving at my mom. She had tears in her eyes. It was as if she knew something that I didn't, the value of having a mother.

I wanted the plane to leave because I was so excited to see America; in my mind, life was not going to get any better than that. I could see the balcony from the airplane window; my mom was still waiting for us to take off. At that time, I didn't know planes could crash, so I wasn't scared at all of what could have happened to me. I slept for most of the flight, except for when the flight attendant brought me dinner. I was used to eating rice, beans, tasso (fried goat or beef), plantain, and Haitian patties. Still, there was something different about the food the flight attendants were serving. Although I enjoyed eating Haitian food, I always wanted to try something different, but never had the chance at home. We never had enough money to eat at a restaurant. They served rice, chicken, and some salad, which I was used to eating, but the airplane food smelled and tasted totally different from what I was used to. It tasted good.

When the plane landed, the airport was confusing. I had never been in such a big airport before, and I didn't know how to speak English. Sheila and I decided to follow everyone else. We were sure some of them had been to the United States before. There, we had our fingerprints taken. I wasn't sure why.

I was happy when I saw Micho; he had come to get us with a friend. I was delighted when I got to see Massachusetts. I stared at those buildings as if I had come from the jungle or something. It felt good to know that I had a dad; I figured if he'd sent for me all the way from Haiti, he had to have some kind of love for me. He had to have missed me to want me to live with him in another country. Many Haitian parents, mostly fathers, forgot their children once they left Haiti; they preferred to get a new spouse and have a new family. The kids born outside of Haiti were treated as if they were more special than those born in Haiti. Dad took care of all of us, made sure all of us went to school, had food on the table, and filed for us to get our green cards. From the day I was born, everything he did included us. Whatever money he made went toward our care. When I lived in Haiti, my mom used to say that he got off work at two in the morning and went back to work again that same morning, just a couple of hours later, with no time to really rest. I was always in bed by 8 or 9 p.m. at the latest. I wondered how he felt during those times.

We drove for thirty to forty-five minutes before reaching our new home in Salem, Massachusetts, a small town outside of Boston. It must have been close to midnight when we arrived home. That same night, we visited my dad's girlfriend, Nadia, a middle-aged woman, probably in her mid-forties. She was tall, slim, and light-skinned with curly hair. She was also from Haiti. She lived with her mother and her two children. There, we got to eat fish with plantain. I had never eaten that late before, so I couldn't finish my food. It felt so good to see Micho eat the rest of my plantain when I couldn't finish it. That night, I went to the bathroom to wash my hands; I had never seen a faucet with two knobs. The faucets I used in Haiti had one knob and the water was either warm or cold depending on the temperature outside. I didn't know what C or H meant, so I turned H. I got burned from the hot water and wished someone had told me the difference that night. I hated to learn things the hard way.

I met Nadia's two children, Jephte and Esther. Esther was closer to my age, around fourteen years old, and Jephte was close to Paul's age. They were both eighteen years old. Everyone was so lovely—at least they were trying to be since it was our first day in America.

We got some lectures, of course. Things like, "You guys are so lucky to be here; listen to your dad; don't worry, you'll be able to speak English like an American very soon. This is a dangerous country; this land is very slippery; blah, blah, blah."

We then went to our new house where Paul, Sheila, Micho, and I would live.

CHAPTER 2

LIVING IN AMERICA

We lived on the first floor of a two-story house that was old, but comfortable. There were three bedrooms. I shared the one all the way in the back with Sheila; Paul shared the one next to it with Micho, and the other room was left empty so Micho could rent it to someone else. Although Micho didn't make a lot of money, we had a big living room with hardwood floors and a beautiful dining room right next to it. We had plenty of space to play around, not to mention the view from the windows. Our house bordered a railroad track, so it was tough to fall asleep at night as the trains came late at night and left early in the morning.

Occasionally, Nadia took us to the mall to show us what we had been missing when we lived in Haiti. I remember the first day we had Chinese food. Fried rice and fried chicken was the one dish most Haitians ordered. It became my second favorite food after Haitian food. Within a few weeks of living in Salem, our lives changed. Nadia started giving us at least one lecture a week about cooking, cleaning, and things that weren't really important at the time, at least not to me. We visited Nadia often because there was no place else to go since we were new to the area and we didn't know anybody. My dad had registered us for school, but we hadn't yet started attending classes.

Since our house didn't have a washing machine or dryer, we used to wash our clothes at the local laundromat. Once a week, we loaded the car and drove to the laundromat. There, we would spend what felt like hours washing and drying our clothes. Sometimes, we met other Haitians and their children. Micho was always excited to meet other Haitians. He never failed to tell them that we had just come from Haiti, and the strangers would tell us how lucky we were to be in the United States. Every now and then, he would give us a few cents to buy chips from the vending machines. Those machines could give out the exact change, which was always fascinating to me.

A trip to Nadia's house could be fun and painful at the same time. It was fun hanging out with Esther and Jephte, because we got to meet their friends. Whenever we visited their house, they would translate for us while we watched television. Some days we would visit Nadia and we would sit in the kitchen and talk for hours. Nadia lived in a one-story house, and each of her kids had their own room. We often sat in the kitchen during our visits. Every now and then, we would sit in the family room to watch television.

Micho visited Nadia almost every day on his way home from work. She used to feed him dinner before we moved to the United States. One day, Micho came home with some food from Nadia's house; it was a bowl of meat with sauce.

"You see how this food looks?" he asked in Haitian Creole. "You need to learn to cook like Nadia."

I had no idea where that came from, but there wasn't really anything to say other than, "Okay." Over time, the negative comments became more frequent. Our house had a small kitchen and a decent-sized dining room that overlooked the street. I cooked most days because Sheila didn't like to. My cooking was decent, but not as good as Nadia's, I'll admit. After cooking, Sheila and I would have to set the table for Micho and put each dish in a separate bowl. We would then have to add one empty plate with a fork, knife, and spoon beside it. Micho would then eat and give us feedback.

Some days, he said the food was too little. Other days, he complained we gave him too much. Some days, the rice was not cooked properly, and the next day it would be too mushy. The beans sauce was sometimes too salty or too watery.

"You need to visit Nadia more so she can teach you how to cook."

I started to miss my mom, wishing that I was still living in Haiti, where my priority used to be school. I missed the hugs and kisses she gave me every day when I got home. I missed the times I used to sit on the floor in front of her so she could play with my hair and massage my scalp. We could not talk to my mom very often because it would cost too much money.

Soon it was time for us to go to school, but we didn't go shopping for supplies. Micho didn't have enough money to care and shop for all of us, so he bought us clothes from the thrift shop. You see, even though Micho worked two jobs, he made less than twenty thousand dollars a year. That's when we started wearing pants. We never wore pants in Haiti; it was part of our religious beliefs.

"It's going to be very cold soon, the weather's not like Haiti. You will get arthritis if you wear skirts," Nadia said.

Nadia even offered to get my ears pierced so I could look cute, but I refused; I thought I looked cute without earrings. Micho went to work before we woke up. Yet, every morning he boiled plantains and made some sauce with hotdogs that he left for us on the stove. He attended an English Second Language night school twice a week, and he always took us whenever they had a party. He always told us that he drove an ugly car and worked in a kitchen so we wouldn't have to.

Micho had two jobs. In the morning, he worked at a hotel's kitchen, and in the afternoon as a janitor at an elementary school. He told us that we had to go to college; it was the only way we were going to get respect. He wanted us to be the ones behind the desk instead of emptying the trash in the office.

"I never want you guys to do this type of work," he would say. "You have to go to school to have a good job like the Americans." He told us, "Stay in school" and "Don't have a boyfriend until you have your degree; men will respect you for it."

"Trust me when I say this because I'm a man. Men only want one thing from you, and once they get it, they'll leave," he said to Sheila and me. "I love you guys, I love all my children. If I didn't, I would not have brought you to America. Don't be like the American girls here who don't listen to their parents and walk around half-naked. You guys have to be different, know that you came here for a better life."

So, I went to middle school, feeling uncomfortable in my new pants. I caught the school bus one block from my house. Sheila and Paul went to high school, so we didn't catch the same bus in the morning. Although Paul was eighteen years old at the time, he was still allowed to attend high school so he could get his diploma. He was placed in the tenth grade so he could have enough time to learn English. School in Haiti last more than twelve years, so it's not uncommon for Haitians to move to the United States and enter high school at eighteen, or even nineteen in some cases.

Middle school was a headache.

My first teacher was Mrs. Smith. She was tall, slim, and blonde. I liked her; she had a unique way of teaching us English. She used a lot of pictures to teach us. The first thing I had to learn was the pledge of allegiance. It wasn't hard, but I didn't have a clue what I was repeating. We had to put our hand over our hearts. In Haiti, we used to salute the flag by sticking our right arm out straight and singing the Haitian National Anthem. Mrs. Smith used pictures to teach us the daily weather. She would open the blinds and ask us to match the weather outside with her pictures. So, I learned that it was sunny when the sun was out. It was raining when water fell from the sky, and it was cloudy when we could not see the sun. I learned the alphabet, colors, numbers, and so forth.

I had to get free lunch because Micho didn't make enough money. I wasn't sure why, but my name was not on the list when I got to the cash register the first day. The lady stared at me when I told her I didn't have any money; I was not sure what I was telling her. I knew what I wanted to say, but I must have pronounced every single word as if I was speaking Haitian Creole.

She let me go with the food even though my name was not on the list, not that I understood her. I did appreciate the hand gestures pointing me to the door of the cafeteria. Lunch period used to be my favorite part of the day since nothing the teachers said registered with me. At least I could take a break from trying to understand everyone and eat a meal in peace.

Math was always one of my favorite subjects. My math teacher, Mr. Kris, was pretty cool. He was bald and had a big belly. One day, we had to do division in class and for homework. I barely understood what Mr. Kris was doing on the board; everything was so backward, but I did notice that we had the same answers. In Haiti, the divisor goes on the right side. The remainder goes directly under the dividend. The students have to perform the subtractions mentally. When I submitted my homework the next day, he couldn't understand how I'd reached the right answer without following the directions he gave. He decided to send me to the board to do a problem, so I did it the Haitian way without all the extra details. Then I had to explain what I did, but I couldn't because my English was so limited. I remember other kids in the classroom getting mad because I got the answer using a technique that they couldn't understand. A few students even told Mr. Kris that I shouldn't get credit because I couldn't explain what I did; some of them were Haitians themselves. When it was time to repeat the numbers, I couldn't count past ten, so when I got to eleven, I kept saying "one, one." Mr. Kris told me it was eleven; he taught me how to count that day. I got terrible looks because other kids found it unfair that I couldn't count but could do division. I found it weird that those kids thought my brain didn't work properly because I couldn't speak their English.

Soon fall and winter came, and I hated it. I thought the summer months were cold until that first winter and I had to stand at the bus stop every morning. Although our house was beautiful, it was pretty old, and the heat didn't work properly for some reason. Sometimes Sheila and I slept with our coats on so we could keep warm during the night. Waking up to shower in the morning was the worst part. It was so cold.

I hated that school bus; everyone took pleasure in me not being able to speak English. The kids were also loud and seldom listened to the bus driver. One afternoon, someone slapped my butt as I was getting off the school bus in front of my house. Everyone started laughing when I turned to ask who had slapped me in Haitian Creole. The closest guy to me was Haitian-American, and he was also laughing, so I figured he was the culprit. I told Micho about it. That afternoon, Micho went to his parents' house and spoke to his mom. Sheila also told Nadia's son, Jephte, what had happened. Jephte was always happy to protect me. I guess he saw me as a little sister since our parents were dating. I found out the next day that the boy's sister had threatened to get me beat up in school because his mom beat him after my dad complained to her. Still, his sister squashed the idea after Jephte threatened to hurt her brother.

Our first Thanksgiving was okay. Growing up in Haiti, my mom often cooked a feast on January 2nd, which is called Ancestry Day. It's a way to honor those who died to gain independence from France. The meal usually included turkey, rice, and beet salad, which was similar to a potato salad but with beets added. For our first Thanksgiving, we went to Nadia's house. She had other relatives over to celebrate the big day. Nadia's mother made the roasted turkey, which was fascinating to see, because growing up, my mom always cut our turkey up. At our first Thanksgiving, we were the only young people there who could not communicate in English, so it was pretty awkward and made us feel like outsiders.

When the food was ready, everyone ate in the dining room, which had around eight to ten chairs, but Paul, Sheila, and I ate at the small table in the kitchen because there was not enough room at the big table for us.

Months passed, and it was warm again. It was toward the end of the school year, and the school was going have a picnic at a place that had a pool. I wanted to buy a bathing suit and asked Micho for thirty dollars.

"I don't have any right now, maybe next week," he said.

Next week would have been too late, but I couldn't tell him that. He was the only one working and taking care of three kids. "Why can't my mom live with us?" I asked. I figured if my mom lived with us and worked, that would be two incomes instead of one. Although my dad worked two jobs, his income still put us below the poverty line. I figured I could definitely get the things that I needed or wanted, like a bathing suit, if my mom was here to work too.

So, he gave me the answer that I wasn't really looking for.

"I don't owe anything to your mom. After all, I am not the only man she has been with, and if the others didn't do anything for her, then why should I?"

Ouch! I thought that was too much information, but pretended like I never heard it. It would have been too painful for me to process, and any answer from me would have made him angrier. She waited for him for seven years; she was faithful to him. Why would he treat her this way? Sheila and I still had contact with my mom, but it wasn't regular because of costs. I don't think we spoke with her more than once per month, but we wrote letters to one another. That was before the Haiti post office was destroyed in the earthquake. All the hopes that I had about my mother coming to the United States were gone; she wasn't following me unless Sheila or I made it happen. But how could I? I was only a child.

One night, Nadia's daughter, Esther, was braiding Sheila's hair. Sheila was two years older than Esther. I guess she wasn't keeping her head straight because Esther hit her on the head with the hairbrush. Sheila was probably seventeen years old at the time. She was basically a young woman, but there was not a thing she could do about it. When Sheila told Micho what happened that night, nothing was done about it. Sheila was supposed to let it slide.

"You guys are new here; you have to remain a part of this family if you want to make it in this country," Micho said.

What family? It wasn't like he and Nadia were married.

We sat in Nadia's kitchen one afternoon, eating, when she had an excellent idea for Paul.

"Paul, I think it would be better if you dropped out of high school."

Paul was in the tenth or eleventh grade at the time and barely spoke English.

"You're not doing anything better with your life, you can't learn, and your dad has bills that need to be paid. Besides, you'll have money to buy nice clothes, and girls will like you because you'll be cuter."

"No, thanks," Paul said. "I'd rather finish school and then get a full-time job."

When Micho came home that night, he decided to talk with Paul while we were eating dinner.

"Paul!" he said. "I just came from Nadia's house, and she gave me a great idea. I think it will be better if you drop out of school and get a job during the day. You can help me with the bills since you're not doing well in school anyway."

"No," Paul said. "The school is free of charge, and I'm going to finish."

The same person who encouraged us to stay in school so we could get a good job was willing to take his son out of school because somebody told him so. Micho never touched that subject again, since it wasn't his idea in the first place, plus he couldn't find Paul a full-time job. I guess his mind was too weak to make his own decisions, so he did whatever his girlfriend said. Maybe he didn't know how to raise kids, and he thought his girlfriend could help since she was both a woman and a mother. I wished he loved us the way he loved Nadia's family. We started visiting Nadia less frequently.

One evening, Micho came home and had a new request for Paul. Nadia had requested that Paul come over and cut her grass going forward, and Micho agreed.

"Why doesn't Jephte cut it?" Paul asked.

"Because I say so," Micho said.

Jephte and Paul were the same age, so why would Nadia or my dad want Paul to cut Nadia's grass when there was another young man living in her house? Unfortunately, Micho was too blind to see the injustice directed at his kids. Not only did Paul not cut Nadia's grass, he never stepped another foot inside Nadia's house again after that incident.

One night, Micho came home from work and called a family meeting. He wanted to know why we'd stopped visiting Nadia. We all sat in the living room to discuss the situation. Micho explained to us how hard he had worked to get us to the United States. He wasn't like other fathers since he didn't leave us in Haiti. All he wanted was for us to show some gratitude toward him and Nadia's family because apparently Nadia and her family helped us get to the States. I wasn't sure how she was involved since they were not married. I sat in front of my father and listened to him lecture us with hate in his voice. The sound of his voice pierced my heart that night. That night, he called us hypocrites for not visiting Nadia. He said Nadia was right and that Paul was dumb and unable to learn. We would never be anything in life unless we bowed to Nadia. The negativity was multiplying quickly. It was overwhelming at times. I thought to myself, *Why didn't Nadia love us the way she loved Micho?* Or, at least, the way she pretended to love him.

Since Jephte was old enough to drive, his car insurance was under Micho's name—for whatever reason—not his mother's. Although Paul was over eighteen years old at the time, Micho made it very clear that he would never sign for a driver's permit or obtain car insurance for any of us. It was just too risky. Although Paul was old enough to get his own driver's license, he could have used Micho's help with driving lessons and car insurance. At seventeen years old, Sheila was also old enough to get her driver's permit, and Micho could have helped. Micho would not take the risk for his own children, but he took it for another man's child.

I started to hate my new house. I began to hate my father's girlfriend for what she was doing to us indirectly. He changed from a caring father to a mean person. He had new rules about the fridge; we weren't allowed to drink from half the drinks in there. For instance, there were two gallons of milk—one for "the children" and the other for Micho. If our milk was finished, we weren't allowed to drink any of his. He would always know, even if we took a little bit, since he used a marker on the gallon to mark the amount he had left. He also wrote his name on his gallon.

"You guys finish yours too quickly," he would say if we drank some. "This one's mine."

Paul found a new way of dealing with the situation. Micho would only know we drank from his gallon if the amount left was lower than the marker, so Paul poured water in there to match the marker. Sometimes we put too much water, and Micho would notice that the taste wasn't the same.

"Who did this to me?" Micho asked one day. "The milk tastes like water."

We all answered that we didn't know and that we hadn't touched it.

We drank Kool-Aid while Micho drank orange juice with his meals. We mostly ate rice and beans. Sometimes we ate cornmeal with bean sauce.

"Nadia said you guys eat too much," Micho told us one afternoon. "From now on, you guys will eat one plantain each, because we don't have enough money."

I was very confused by his words because the government gave Micho food stamps to pay for our groceries. However, we only went grocery shopping once a month, and once our food was gone, we had to wait for the next distribution. We lived like strangers, even though we were supposed to be a family.

If Micho washed the pots or his dishes, we would know by the signs he would post around the house. There were signs everywhere—in the kitchen, the hallway, next to the bedrooms—to tell us that the pots were cleaned and that he'd cleaned them. I guess washing his own dishes after eating was also a favor to us.

"You guys will never be able to keep a man," Micho used to say to Sheila and me. "Your husbands will beat you because you can't cook. What did your mother teach you in Haiti?" he would say weekly.

At that point, I was not even thinking of having a husband. If having a family meant being so unhappy, I didn't want one. And if I had kids with a guy, I would never fully trust him or his family with them the way my mom trusted Micho with us. If I ever got married, I would want to be with someone who loved me, not someone who was after me because of what he thought I could do for him, like cooking his meals or ironing his clothes. I figured if a guy loved me, he would love my children as well. Sometimes I used to think Micho would have been kinder to us if he liked our mothers.

During one of our rare visits to Nadia's house, she took the opportunity to give us some advice on our future in regards to education. On the surface, it seemed like the most loving conversation one person could have with another. For someone to take the time to give another advice on education made it seem loving. But it was anything but loving. Bottom line was we would never be able to go to college because Micho didn't have money to pay our tuition. At the time, Jephte had already started college, so we figured Nadia knew what she was talking about.

"I pay cash for Jephte's education," Nadia said.

And so I thought I would never amount to anything because there was no way my dad would be able to pay for my education, not while he was making under twenty thousand dollars a year and taking care of three kids. There was no way Sheila would ever become a doctor. That dream was dead. Had we stayed in Haiti, she could have attended the public medical school for free. I always wanted to be a lawyer, but that dream was dead too. How could I ever realize it if I needed to pay tens of thousands of dollars to get a degree? The words that originally sounded like advice were actually filled with poison and lies.

"If you guys want to make it, you have to do what you're told and stay under Nadia's wings," Nadia's mother said. "She knows better and can help you."

Everything revolved around the family—Nadia's family. It didn't matter that I was a child and that I required love and attention. If I wanted to be loved, I had to kiss butts. I didn't have the right to choose; I wasn't my own person anymore. Whatever Micho or Nadia said was final, even if it hurt.

I started to get mad at my mom for letting me come without her. She was the only one who ever protected me completely. Soon, I realized that I wasn't protected anymore. Although we were still writing letters to one another, we were not telling her everything that was happening because we did not want her to worry.

There was a big gap inside my heart. I was empty, and there was no one to talk to. Micho's lectures became more frequent.

They were almost expected after a while, and they all revolved around Nadia. The only people close to me were Nadia's kids, but I couldn't trust them. I didn't know what was inside their hearts. There's a Haitian saying that goes *a tiger's child is a tiger*; it might be small, but it will grow up to be a vicious tiger just like its parents. I guess that's why I couldn't trust Nadia's kids completely. I saw their mother as a tiger, and in my eyes, they were just younger tigers waiting to grow into big ones.

I was in art class one day when a skinny Puerto Rican kid named Jose would not stop bothering me. Although I didn't understand English well, I knew when someone was being annoying. I threw all my paint on his face and clothes. Someone later translated for me that he was going to stab me the next day. The last thing I wanted was to get stabbed in America. That night, I sat on my bed, staring at the wall, thinking of how I was going to skip school the next day.

"Cynthia, à quoi tu penses comme ça?" Micho asked.

He wanted to know what I was thinking.

"Rien," I replied. I told him I was not thinking about anything.

I prayed that night that God would make Jose forget me. My prayer was answered because the next day, he looked at me and walked away as if nothing had happened.

Months later, I still refused to speak English; I wrote it well but I could not speak it. Since my writing was so good, I was promoted to a higher English Second Language class. I was in my writing class one day when I was pulled out by a French teacher who wanted to know why I refused to speak English.

"Your writing is excellent," she said. "Why won't you speak English?"

She didn't understand. If I was doing it on purpose, she said, I would only hurt myself because she would put me back in level one. I tried to explain to her that I really could not speak it, so I was making the choice to listen instead of just speaking words that made no sense. I thought if I learned English the wrong way, I would speak improper English forever, and I didn't want that. The only time I think I ever responded to the teacher was when she took attendance. Whenever I heard, "Cynthia Josaphat," I would say, "present" without pronouncing the letter "t."

In Physical Education (PE), I met Diana. She had just come from Haiti, like me, and spoke very little English, so we clicked pretty well. Because of Diana, PE was one of my favorite classes, although I was terrible at playing sports. It was the only class that I could not get an A in since I always got shortness of breath from jumping too much. On the other hand, Diana was great at playing volleyball; she always seemed to be able to hit the ball hard enough to win. The teacher always placed her in the last row so she could catch the ball. She even got a presidential certificate from President Bill Clinton.

PE was also where I met Pierre, the guy who thought of me as the prettiest girl in the entire school. He once wrote me a love letter in French and placed it on my desk. I found it so funny that this guy was interested in me; I had seen so many pretty girls in school with long hair and big butts, so I didn't understand what he saw in me. I later told everyone in the class that he had written me a letter and let others read it. When I looked into his eyes, I could see that I had embarrassed him, but I did not care because I wasn't interested in boys at the time. Pierre must have chased me every day for months, but I never saw anything in him. He even bought me flowers for Valentine's Day; the school sold them for a dollar. But I still felt nothing.

I wasn't going to wind up like my mother and choose the wrong man. I was determined to do better for myself. My mother had made terrible choices as far as men were concerned.

CHAPTER 3:

MY MOTHER'S LIFE

My mother was a homemaker. I heard that, as a young girl, my mom was the prettiest of four sisters; every guy on the block wanted her. From the way she curled her dark, silky hair, to her oriental eyes, her peach skin, and the way she carried herself, including her cooking skills, everything about her was almost designed to attract a man. She didn't get to finish school. She blamed it on the fact that she was not raised by her mother. She always told me I was going to be just like her and choose the wrong man in life.

My mom was a church girl until she got pregnant with Sheila. She was expelled from the church for having a baby out of wedlock. She had been raised by her stepmother, Jesula. Her mom sent her and her older brother, Anel, to live with my grandfather after their divorce. She was five years old at the time. She didn't see her mother again until she was in her mid-thirties. Jesula once told me that she was unable to have children for many years, but God had mercy on her because she was so good to her stepchildren. Jesula was also religious, but my grandfather was not. He preferred to smoke and drink liquor in his spare time.

Jesula was technically my step-grandmother, but she was my grandmother in every way possible. I remember lying on her lap so she could braid my hair as a little girl. Because my mom's house shared a wall with hers, we visited her often. She used to tell us Bible stories about the second coming. She taught us Bible verses. She loved to sing. She used to sing Christian songs to us, especially on the weekends. She sang so loud that it was hard to miss the gold tooth barely hanging from the front of her mouth. The best part about visiting her was the stories she told us, but I also loved her spaghetti with turkey and red sauce. Never in my life have I met anyone that came even close to making a spaghetti dish like Jesula. I loved her very much.

Jesula wanted Micho to marry my mom because of religion. As for my grandfather, he never forgave or liked Micho for not making an honest woman out of my mother before she gave birth to Sheila.

Nirlande was my mom's name; I'm not sure who she was named after. She loved Micho. She stayed with him despite my grandfather's disapproval, and not only did they have me out of wedlock too, they also had my stillborn little brother. I don't know why, but my mom just seemed to love that man no matter what he did to her. She always shut her eyes as if she were blind. That's one thing I didn't like about her, although I loved her to pieces. She could let a man and his family manipulate her because she believed in love.

I think the month Sheila and I left her for the United States was the last time my parents spoke. She was dropped like a dirty bag of laundry, something that wasn't needed anymore. Maybe he thought she wasn't good enough. There was never a word about her in our new house unless it was negative; it was like she never existed. I still wonder how she felt when he stopped talking to her; she must have been embarrassed and hurt. With all her family watching, they told her Micho was no good for her, but she didn't listen. My grandparents never really cared for my dad because he didn't show any intention of getting married to her. On top of that, he hid Paul's birth from them. Paul and Sheila were born less than one year apart. They warned my mom that Micho was bad news, but she didn't listen. She hung in there for over seventeen years and ended up with nothing.

I think it was a year after we got to Salem that Sheila got a part-time job at a laundromat. I don't think she made more than forty dollars a week from that job. She used to send some of that money to my mom in Haiti.

"I don't want you to send any more money to your mom," Dad said to her. "We need the money right here to pay bills."

I was shocked and angry at the same time. I thought about my mother wasting all that time on a man and ending up with that type of inhumane treatment. I didn't think it was fair. Just because he'd dropped her didn't mean we had to follow in his footsteps. She was the woman who'd carried us for nine months inside her womb and had given birth to us. She'd taken care of us when we were sick; she was the only human being who ever loved us unconditionally.

At first, I didn't get it. I used to say to myself that my mom should just get over it and move on to do better. I was too young to understand what it meant to be in love with a man who didn't love you back. My mom never told us what she was feeling inside. She probably thought I was too young to handle it, and she was right—I was.

Then Sheila said to me that Micho had married another woman in the United States while we lived in Haiti. That was, of course, before he married my mother during his trip to Haiti. I even got to see the pictures. What shocked me the most was the type of wedding that she had. The woman looked so beautiful in those pictures; she wore a lovely white wedding dress with a white veil. The reception was splendid—a real one, not a doll's party. Maybe my mom didn't deserve a beautiful wedding. Perhaps this lady wasn't taking his nonsense or his family's rubbish like my mom did. I never understood why my mom agreed to have the wedding in the first place. Maybe something was done to her self-esteem during those years she spent with him. Micho and the woman divorced before we moved to America.

From what I heard, he hit my mom when things didn't go his way when I was a little girl. I can only recall one incident when it happened, however. I was too young to remember the whole thing, but I know the neighbors came into the house and took us children out. The violence didn't happen again because my mom's little brother, Ralph, threatened to kill Micho if he ever hit his sister again. To this day, I still don't know what she saw in him. Maybe it was the smell of his cologne or the fact that he was fluent in French and had a job when they met. Perhaps she wanted a man who could provide a home for her and her children. I often asked myself if she really thought he loved her or if she just made herself believe that he did.

I was probably nine or ten years old when my mom asked me to do something that I'll never forget. She had cramps that day and was desperate for some pills to make the pain go away.

She wanted to buy a pill called "Saridon." It cost no more than fifty centimes in Haitian currency, which was precisely ten cents in U.S. currency. I don't think she had any money because she couldn't buy it and she was in a lot of pain. She asked me to take fifty cents from her neighbor's purse to buy her the pill. My mom was no thief; she had class and respected people, and she had me do it out of desperation. She didn't do it to improve our lifestyle or to eat; it was to make her pain go away. That's how unhappy she was at times, and loneliness was her best friend. She never said it, but I could see it in her eyes that she was so alone. Sheila and I were the two people who kept her going. If she had five gourdes, she gave it to us to buy whatever we wanted to eat and starved herself.

One day we came home from school, and no food was prepared in the house that day. Unlike the United States, most Haitians go to the market and cook daily; no leftovers are kept for the next day. Our neighbor, Sabrina, gave her a bowl of food. Mom split it in half, and she said to Sheila and me, "Each one of you gets one, and go study your lessons when you're done." That day, I promised myself I would never have her life. I would work hard to make sure there was always food on my table, and I would make her proud of me.

I missed my mother. It was hard being so far away from her with so little contact, and soon, I would really need her.

CHAPTER 4

SURGERY

Because of my constant shortness of breath in gym class, I was told by the school nurse to bring a letter from a cardiologist. As a child, my mom always took me to prayer meetings on Saturdays. There, everyone sat on the ground on a blanket on top of the mountain. Female attendees covered their heads with a scarf and prayed for an extended period of time. I always hated going to that place. My first reason was the fact that we had to walk a lot to get there. I'm not sure how long it would take us to get there because I was so young, but it must have taken at least an hour, walking in the sun. The fact that it took place on top of a mountain did not make things easier.

I also had to keep my eyes closed the entire time during prayers, or my mom would pinch me or tell me that I wouldn't get a popsicle that day. As much as I hated going to that place for half the day, getting a popsicle at the end of it was the best part. There, everyone would start praying at the same time, really loud. Some would cry because it was the place people went when something was really wrong. Others caught the Holy Spirit. Many people claimed their prayers had been answered and gave testimonies. So my mom had hope that I would be cured too.

I was born with a congenital heart defect. My heart rate was usually around one hundred twenty beats per minute (as opposed to the normal sixty to one hundred beats per minute). I often vomited when riding in a car, and I had trouble breathing if I got wet in the rain. Running was never an option for me. My parents knew of my heart condition since the day I was born. In fact, the doctor who delivered me used to visit me just to see how I was doing. I used to see a cardiologist with my dad when he lived in Haiti, but the visits stopped after he left the country. My mother believed I could be cured through prayer, and so she always requested the person in charge of the prayer service to put her hand on my chest and pray.

"Please pray that she's cured; she has a bad heart," my mom would tell them.

For years, my mom believed that I was cured, and I trusted her. But now, I didn't have a choice but to see the cardiologist if I wanted to return to school the following year.

"She needs to have an operation," the cardiologist told Micho.

I was just sitting there like an idiot, thinking, *Is this guy serious? I'm cured. How dare he?*

The doctor confirmed that I had a congenital heart defect. A valve was not operating correctly. There was a hole in my heart. I had a heart murmur. They needed to fix it. They needed to close a hole. It was a complicated situation for my fourteen-year-old mind, but I knew the doctors were right. I used to get very sick at least once a month when I lived in Haiti. I used to have trouble breathing at least one entire day each month. Only at night would things go back to normal.

My mom never took me to the hospital; she didn't like doctors. I don't know if it was because we were poor or because she simply didn't believe in them. She used to get some specific leaves from a tree, boil them, and I would drink the tea. To me, that was the way life was supposed to be. I would get sick, she would make me tea, and I would feel better. Life went on. There were times when I used to be gasping for air, like my airway was blocked, but I still never went to a hospital for it. I got used to it, so I never thought of having surgery. My mom always told me that God had cured me; she'd been praying about it since the day I was born. She left everything up to Him, especially my health.

The cardiologist performed an echocardiogram that day. He must have called at least five other doctors, and one by one, they confirmed what he said—there was a hole in my heart, and I needed surgery. That day was such an embarrassment. I didn't have big breasts, but I did have two bumps on my chest. It was not a good feeling to have so many people check to see if the previous one was right. Even at fourteen, I looked more like a nine-year-old American child. I was short, skinny, and underdeveloped for my age.

One day I was cooking in the kitchen. Paul was playing music in the living room, and Sheila was cleaning our bedroom located in the back of the house. All of a sudden, fire shot up from the stove toward the ceiling. I screamed, and Paul rushed over. He turned the knobs off, but the fire continued to rise. We screamed "Fire!" and ran. Sheila exited the house through the bedroom window. Together we ran down the street screaming, "Fire!" Thankfully, someone called the fire department and they showed up in minutes. They were able to cut off the gas and deemed the house unsafe.

Micho found another place for us to live. It was located a couple miles from where we had been living. It was the bottom floor of a split-level house. A family lived upstairs, and another Haitian family lived downstairs. The downstairs level had four rooms, two on each side of the house; a large kitchen was in the middle. The family lived in two rooms with their two children, and Micho subleased the other two rooms for the four of us. Micho and Paul stayed in the smaller room. Micho used a curtain to split the bigger room into our bedroom and our living room.

As we got closer to the date of the surgery, I started wondering who was going to care for me. I lived in a house with two other kids and Micho, no mother. The last thing I needed was to be helpless. Not that I had a choice; since Micho was my legal guardian, it was up to him whether I had the operation.

I remember going back to the cardiologist's office. That was the day Micho had to sign the papers, and the cardiologist gave us a time for the operation. My doctor's office was not too far from my house, but I had to have the operation at a bigger hospital in Boston. I remember the doctor asking Micho where my mom was.

"She's going to need someone to take care of her," he said. He gave Micho some documents to send to my mom in Haiti; they were supposed to help her get a visa to come take care of me after the operation since I was still a minor. Micho did not give the letter to my mom. She never went to the embassy, and she never came.

I had many mixed emotions about the surgery. I was pissed that my mom was not going to be there to take care of me, but then I started to like the idea of having heart surgery. I wanted to get away from that house. If someone was not going to get me out of there, that surgery was my only way out, even temporarily.

I got baptized at my church five days before having the operation. I wanted to save my soul just in case I died on the operating table. I also asked the pastor to pray for me so that everything would go well; I have no idea why I asked him to do so. I wanted to survive and die at the same time. I wanted to test my faith, so I asked God to cure me without the operation. As the number one doctor in the universe, I wanted Him to perform the operation without cutting me open. I honestly believed that I was not going to have the operation anymore since I asked God to do it Himself. I prayed nonstop, and my faith was so strong that I believed I was cured.

"I'm not going to have the operation anymore," I told my mom over the phone one day.

She was excited, of course.

"Why? Did Micho change his mind?" she asked.

"No," I said, "God cured me."

"Blessed be His name," she said. "How's Micho doing?" she asked.

I wasn't sure what to tell her. Micho wanted nothing to do with her. It was almost like he hated her. Like he never loved her. She wanted to know how Micho was, she wanted to know everything about him; it seemed as if she still loved him. She didn't seem to know how to let go. I didn't understand why she even cared; they had not spoken in about a year.

It was time for me to have the operation; the procedure was set for Monday morning. Micho took me to the hospital on Sunday evening. Sheila's godfather visited that morning to wish me well. Our neighbors also visited to wish me well. My siblings hugged and kissed me goodbye with sad looks on their faces, as if I wasn't coming back. Not that I cared—I sincerely believed the operation was no longer needed. I didn't want to return to that house either way. It would've been a peaceful way to die anyway, with no pain and no memory of it whatsoever. That night, the surgeon explained to me that I was going to have tubes in my mouth and nose. He came with pictures and asked me if I wanted to be restrained, but I said no.

After the doctor left, a nurse came and took me to get another echocardiogram. I was waiting for them to tell me that I was cured, but she took me back to my room in a wheelchair. On our way back, we got stuck inside the elevator, and we must have spent at least fifteen minutes in there before someone came and helped. That was my first experience with claustrophobia. It was terrifying. I felt like the walls of the elevator were closing in on me. It was my first night sleeping in a hospital; I thought of all the ghost stories that I had heard in Haiti as a child. I dreamed of ghosts coming to my room and scratching my feet or just sitting next to me and scaring me.

It was around six or seven the next morning when the nurse came and got me. She gave me a pill, which I placed under my pillow. I could never swallow pills. I was placed in an open area with other patients waiting to be taken to their own operating rooms. Everyone had family members holding their hands. I seemed to have been the youngest and only person there alone at the time, with no one to hold my hand. That was even more painful than those days at my so-called home. Tears just kept flowing from my eyes and running to the back of my ears. I was so sad that no words could explain the feelings that I felt inside. I was not angry. I'm not sure I wished for anyone to be next to me. I don't even know what I hoped for at the time; all I know is I was despondent.

In the operating room, a man was in charge of putting all the IVs in my arms. He showed me the two plastic needles he was about to insert inside my veins, and he told me not to move my arm, that it would be over soon. I screamed when the needle got close to my skin. He seemed to be the most sensitive person I had come in contact with since moving to America. As he wiped my tears, he told me not to cry. He then asked me to stare at a bright light and placed a mask over my mouth and nose that smelled like a freezer. I am not sure what happened after that as everything went dark.

I was barely awake a few hours later, with tubes sticking out from all over my body. I heard machines beeping; I had an IV with blood flowing through my veins, and another with clear fluid. There was a tube inside my nose that was probably for oxygen, I didn't know for sure. There was another tube inside my mouth, and I am not sure what its purpose was, but there was some type of fluid coming out of it. There was also another tube on my left side near my ribcage. That one had blood flowing on one side and water on the other. I was so miserable—horrible is the only word I can use to describe that day. When I finally woke up from the anesthesia, Daniel, Micho's cousin, who was a nurse, came to visit. I couldn't open my eyes to see, but I could hear him talk. He checked all the machines to make sure the doctors and nurses did what was supposed to be done.

A lady also visited, but I'm not sure who she was. I wanted to scream for someone to hold my hand, but could not. That lady was the only one who thought of holding my hand. A few moments later, she said, "You're going to be okay." At that point, I felt like I could cry. I felt free, tears flowed from my eyes, and I let it all out.

Micho brought Paul and Sheila to visit me, but they didn't stay. I didn't even get to see their faces, but I knew they came because I heard their voices. They also left before I could open my eyes. I wasn't sure what day or time it was, but once again, I had that same sad feeling I'd had before the operation. Here I was alone, with no one to hold my hand and tell me that it was going to be okay. My body was stiff, not painful, but very weird and uncomfortable. Then I thought of the letter the cardiologist gave for my mom to take to the embassy. That letter would have allowed her to apply for a visa to take care of me. I thought of Nadia, who called me a hypocrite for not eating her kids' leftovers, who claimed she loved me so much, the one who was causing my soul to bleed. If only my mom had made it to Salem, she would've been with me at the hospital every second of the day and night. Maybe I was paying for something that my parents—or better yet, my ancestors—did. And then I started to ask myself why Nadia and her family didn't visit me. Why didn't anyone think of visiting me? It was no secret that I was having open heart surgery, and everyone knew about it, yet no one was there. And still, I was supposed to believe that they all loved me—just because they said so.

Everything was going through my mind at the same time, and I felt like I was going crazy. I wasn't sad anymore, I was angry, and I needed to do something quickly before I exploded. There was a tube that kept sliding down my throat every time I swallowed my saliva. It was getting on my nerves, and I wanted to get rid of it, so I pulled it out. Next thing I knew, I was gasping for air. I sat on the bed, unable to speak; the machines were beeping like crazy. Doctors and nurses came from every direction, trying to help. I couldn't even stay still. As much as I wanted to die, I desperately needed to have air flowing through my lungs. I was intubated and could feel air inside my chest. That was one of the most uncomfortable moments of my life.

"Breathe, sweetie, breathe," a nurse kept saying. With God's help, I started to breathe again. I don't think Micho knew about that incident. After all, no one was there to speak to the doctor about my condition after Daniel's visit the day of the operation. I spent seven days in the hospital. Besides Daniel, who visited me once, not one person in Nadia's family visited, not even a phone call. No wonder the nurses didn't care half the time, as one of them left me sitting in a chair for over two hours a day or two after I had the operation. I thought I was going to faint. She was called by a doctor who saw me standing, trying to walk toward the bed with a container that looked like a gallon attached to the tube that was inserted around my ribcage area on my left side.

Sometimes I used to push the "help" button, and no one would come. I even asked for a blanket once and never got it. They had nothing to worry about; it wasn't like I had family members to complain about how they were treating me. Micho revisited a couple of days after the operation; he touched my hair and asked how I was feeling. Micho visited about three times during my one-week stay at the hospital. The pastor of the church and another older lady from the church also visited. She asked if it was okay for her to braid my hair, and I accepted the offer since it had not been done in days. They stayed with me, talked to me, and prayed with me during the time they were there. They waited to leave me until it was time for my chest x-ray.

I was placed in a wheelchair, and the pastor helped put my slippers on. The nurses cheered when they saw my braids. "You look much better now," one of them said. Right after the x-ray was taken, the radiologist told me that I still had a small hole inside my heart, but it might close with time.

I was later placed in a room with another teenage girl. I'm not sure what was wrong with her, but her boyfriend always visited. He only left when visiting hours were over, so the television became my best friend. It was the first time since I was a little girl that I found pleasure in watching cartoons. I was placed on a floor with a game room where other children played. I never stepped foot in that room. I didn't think I belonged there. Although the kids there were sick, I could see how happy they were.

I had much more to think about than my sore skin. I remember lying in bed one night, sobbing because my chest was hurting so much. They had stopped giving me pain medication through an IV. It was like someone was burning me with a hot iron, and I needed it to be taken away. That girl called the nurse, and the nurse tried to give me some pills. I tried, but could not swallow them. She later crushed them and put them in apple sauce, and still, I could not take them because it tasted so bitter. The nurse was so caring and patient; she stayed with me for an extended period of time, begging me to take the painkiller, but I didn't. She later told me that I was the toughest kid she had ever met at that hospital. I was willing to suffer that night instead of taking bitter pills. I'm not sure what time I fell asleep that night, but it took me a few hours.

The day I got out of the hospital was a happy day. The nurses lined up outside my room and in the hallway. They were all cheering, "Cynthia, Cynthia, we're going to miss you." I saw Micho smile. He pushed my wheelchair that day and pulled the car up right in front of the hospital. He opened the door for me to get in and then buckled my seat belt. I was so happy to see my Aunt Claudette from Haiti. She came with her children to take care of me since my mom could not come. She cooked for me, gave me baths daily, did my hair, and gave me love.

I shared a queen-sized bed with Sheila, but after the operation, she decided to let me sleep on the bed alone and slept in the living room. That night I could not fall asleep; my back hurt when I was on my back. My shoulders hurt when I was on my side, and sleeping on my stomach was not even an option. I cried that night that God would take my pain away.

"Help me fall asleep, God," I prayed. The next day I was tired from not sleeping, but I couldn't tell anyone that I didn't sleep because I would then be forced to take painkillers. The surgeon had cut below my underarm on my left side, and the cut stretched at least eight inches up my back, so it was hard for me to do anything with my left arm. My body was still stiff from the stitches and tape on my skin. I wanted so much to stretch, and I did, but then I grimaced, and Aunt Claudette noticed that I still had pain from the operation.

"Cynthia, be careful, honey," she said. For about a week, I had trouble sleeping. I wanted so much for someone to take my pain away. I couldn't tell anyone that I was still in pain because I'd have to take Tylenol or some other painkiller, but at the same time, I wanted it to go away. One afternoon, I fell asleep on the couch as I sat there watching television. It was the first time I'd slept in days. Since the sofa was a little harder than my bed, it gave me better support, and I was more comfortable sleeping there. From that night on, I slept on the couch until I felt like I was ready to sleep in my bed.

It was a Friday night when I finally decided to go back to my bed; I still slept alone. Sheila and Aunt Claudette still slept on the floor. Although I was not in constant pain from the operation anymore, I was still unable to stretch. That night, I lay there thinking how much I wanted to stretch, so I thought of stretching a bit. Just when I was getting ready to move my arms, I heard a voice.

"No," it said. It sounded like it was coming from my dad's room, but when I opened my eyes, my room was pitch dark. I still felt like I had to stretch, so I tried to move my arm again, the left one. I heard the voice again, "No," and someone tapped my leg. I opened my eyes, and the room was dark; I was alone. At that point, I realized that I wasn't alone and that someone from Heaven was watching over me even when I couldn't see Him. I got scared and started shaking, but a few minutes later, my fears went away. I thanked God for being with me, and I prayed that He would take all my pain away; that was the last night my wound or chest hurt nonstop from the operation.

I finally got a visit from Jephte, Nadia, and her mother a few days after I was discharged from the hospital. Jephte told me he had no idea I was having surgery. I guess Nadia and her mother didn't want to waste gas driving to the hospital. By then, it was at least a week and a half after I'd had the operation. I had gone to the park earlier that day; the doctor suggested that I walk to make my heart stronger. The park was located less than a mile from my house.

"Why did you go to the park?" Nadia asked. "You would not have been able to run if there was a shooting," she said.

It wasn't like we lived in a dangerous area. I didn't see how there could be a shooting. I would have had to be a very unlucky person for something like that to happen while I was sick. I looked upset. So instead of asking how I was doing, she proceeded to tell me how ungrateful I was for not appreciating the visit or the advice. *Are you kidding me?* I thought. No one asked how I was, nor did they ask how the operation went. I guess they were happy that I was still alive so they could still have me under their nose to sniff at.

I was so angry that day I could just die.

"You don't understand; we tell you these things because we love you," Micho said.

I didn't see what love had to do with it; I didn't know love could be seen. I thought it was something that I was supposed to feel, but I couldn't feel it no matter how hard I tried. That night I saw tears in Aunt Claudette's eyes while we sat on the bed to talk.

"Your mom loves you guys so much," Aunt Claudette said. "She would've given you guys the world if she could, but she couldn't."

She told us that she wasn't going to tell my mom any of the things she witnessed because she didn't want to break her heart. My mom was Aunt Claudette's favorite sister, and she didn't want to see her more unhappy—or should I say, more miserable—than she already was. A month passed by with my aunt in the house, and things went smoothly; it was like we had a home again. Soon she had to leave; she had to return to work, her kids had to go back to school in Haiti, and the school year was also about to start in Salem. Once again, Sheila, Paul, and I were back in Hell.

CHAPTER 5

LIVING IN HELL

One night my dad came home and said it was time for another family meeting. Nadia had told him something new.

"Sheila, from now on, you're going to have to iron my clothes, no questions asked," he said. "Nadia told me I'm working hard, and you guys need to help. She loves me, and she's always right," he said.

It would not have been a big deal to iron, besides the fact that we were already doing all the chores in the house. A please or thank you would've been nice, but Micho didn't think we deserved such words of gratitude.

Soon Nadia and her family stopped visiting, but they worked through Micho. I called them the "Invisible Hands." They didn't tell us how worthless we were anymore, at least not to our faces. All three of us were breaking down in the house, but we tried as much as possible to stay close and never turned on one another. We made that promise when we saw the wedding pictures of Micho's first marriage and promised each other if he asked who had been snooping through his things, we weren't going to turn each other in. If one of us had to be beaten, we were all going to be beaten. Although the three of us didn't grow up in the same house, we were determined to make the best of what that house had to offer. We stuck together, no matter what. I thought if one of us had to die, all three of us would have had to die.

We kept our word. The day we went through his stuff and discovered his wedding photos, he came home and asked who had gone through his things. We all said we didn't know, so he beat all of us with a long, wooden stick, almost like a baseball bat, but not as thick. He beat Paul with rage as if he had something against him. My brother offered to be beaten in my place since I screamed right after the first hit. It was a horrible day, but no matter what Micho did, we didn't snitch on each other. I think that incident made him and Nadia dislike us even more. We were determined to protect one another, and they hated that with a passion.

One night, I decided to go to a basketball game at school, and a friend's mom dropped us off. Micho called later that night, asking where I'd gone. He knew I was going to the game.

"Where were you?" he asked.

"I went to the game," I replied.

"Well, you didn't go to any game. I just got good information from people who have lived in this country for years, and they told me that there are no games on school nights. You went out with boys and lied."

Sheila and I were both virgins. I had never kissed a boy before and didn't plan on kissing one anytime soon. I was vexed.

They knew that I wasn't sleeping around; they said it to get on my nerves and ruin my reputation. After all, Nadia's kids had to be better than me, so if I went to school, church, and had no boyfriends to sleep with, that made me a good girl, and it wasn't possible because I wasn't supposed to be good. It was Nadia's children's world, not mine. I was fifteen years old when that incident happened. Maybe I didn't know the definition of the word slut, but that was not the behavior of a slut, not in my book.

There was a lecture given almost every night for two years and six months. Very few came directly from Nadia's mouth to us—instead, most were transmitted through Micho. Now, Micho was not a good liar. He would always tell us who told him right before he said it was for our own good.

It was always, "Nadia says you guys overeat. You're wasting food by eating two plantains instead of one. Nadia says the house is too dirty. You guys need to start going to Nadia's house to learn how to cook properly. Nadia says you guys don't visit. You guys don't call. You guys are hypocrites. You'll never make it in this country without Nadia's or her family's help. This land is very slippery. You guys will fall, and they won't be there to help you. Nadia loves you, can't you see that? You guys love your mom's family more than me, why? Your mom's family members haven't done anything for you, but I gave you a green card; you owe everything to me, blah, blah, blah."

I didn't know coming to America was a favor, and I never asked to be born. No one found me in the streets and decided to pick me up; I was raised by the same people who had birthed me. To make things worse, I had a teacher who was getting on my nerves for not wanting to speak English. Though I didn't know how to express myself clearly, I did my best; I could write it, read it, but I could not speak it well. I could not stand that teacher; all we did in that English class was learn how to write in print. I grew up writing in cursive.

Mr. Cheval was his name; he was tall, skinny, and wore ugly glasses. I remember him threatening to call Micho to complain about me sleeping in class. Micho did not give the school our home phone number; instead, he gave them Nadia's phone number. I believed he would call Nadia's because he had done it before, but I didn't care anymore by then. Although I couldn't speak English very well, I could always get my message across if I wanted to.

So I told the teacher that day, "Don't worry, I'm not coming to school anymore because I'm going to die."

I wasn't sure why I said that. I wasn't planning on doing anything, but that's what I felt like saying at the time. It worked, though, as the teacher promised not to call and sent me to another office in the school. I had no idea who that lady was. She asked me to have a seat across from her on a sofa. I didn't understand half the things she was saying to me, as my English was so limited, and I'm sure she knew that because I never saw her again. That was my very first visit with a therapist.

I went home that night and had to cook and do the usual chores. I still hated that house; it made me sick to my stomach. Later that night, I thought that I really did not want to live anymore. The only two people that I could trust were also sick of their own lives, so I kept my business to myself. I must have taken about ten aspirins that night. Even though I hated taking pills and had always had a hard time swallowing them, I found it was much easier to let them soak in orange juice until they melted—which actually made the taste more unbearable. But I was in so much emotional pain that I managed to choke down the pills. I wanted to die, but I didn't want to suffer, so I went to bed. I figured I would die in my sleep, and everything would be over soon.

The next day, my eyes opened in time for school. I was even more pissed because I really didn't want to go to that school; I didn't want to see anyone—they just didn't get it. I found myself crying again that morning because I was alive. Some people were sad because they wanted to live, and life didn't want them, but I was crying because death didn't want me.

That morning I took more pills. I didn't die, but I did get sick at school and vomited in the nurse's office. I didn't tell anyone what happened, but I later had to go to the emergency room for chest pain. Jephte took me, and I remember that day because Nadia's mother was in the same hospital for knee surgery. When I was released that afternoon, I went upstairs to her room, and I noticed Micho was already there.

Why didn't he come downstairs to see me? I asked myself. Sheila was forced to spend a few nights in the hospital with Nadia's mom during the time she spent there. Micho took Sheila to visit me once when I had open heart surgery, but no one ever spent a night with me; it was always just me and my empty room. Now, I know I was young, but I was not stupid. It was all about common sense—knee surgery or heart surgery, which one was more dangerous? Which one was more capable of taking some-one's life? Of course, it wasn't about who was suffering or who was sicker; it was all about who was a human being and who was not. Clearly, I was not seen as human. I couldn't complain, of course, because they had all the power.

The next few months were full of ups and downs. Our relationship with Micho deteriorated. We became less connected, and nothing he did surprised us anymore. We completely stopped visiting Nadia. We rarely spoke to her kids unless it was necessary. Paul, Sheila, and I were in survival mode. We woke up every day and hoped it would go fast enough so we could go back to bed—and do it all over again the next day. At that point, our goal was to survive long enough until we were able to move out of the house. We became each other's support system. We gossiped when we were together and came up with plans on how we would survive however number of months or years we had left with Micho. Some days we all cried together; other days we laughed together. Micho didn't say much to us anymore. He mostly came home, ate, and went to bed. He pretty much ignored us unless Nadia told him to say something to us, which happened pretty often. I wasn't sure if he loved us, but I could tell he didn't like us.

A few months after heart surgery, it was time to move again. This time we moved into a two-story colonial style house. A Haitian family lived on the second floor with their teenage children. There were at least four people living there. The first floor had two bedrooms with a large living room, dining room, and a kitchen. The house had a large driveway, a front yard, and a backyard. We lived on the first floor. Sheila and I shared a small room in the back. Another lady rented the bigger bedroom from the landlord. She was related to the people who lived upstairs, but she wanted her privacy. My dad shared the living room area with Paul. He used a curtain as a wall so visitors could not see inside. The dining area became our living room. Another Haitian family lived in the basement with their teenage daughter and young son.

By then, Paul had gotten a job at a Haitian bakery where he would bake bread and Haitian patties. Every now and then, we would order pizza for supper. Things seemed to have calmed down a bit. Micho seemed to have accepted the fact that we wanted nothing to do with Nadia or her family. And we accepted the fact that he would never love us the way we needed to be loved. So, I continued to cook our meals, and Sheila cleaned our house. Paul mostly served as our protector, sharing his one-hundred-dollar paychecks with us after he gave Micho a portion of it.

Nearly one year after I had heart surgery, I visited my mom's cousin, Martin, in Atlanta, Georgia; he was my mom's first cousin. He wanted me to come so much that he paid for my plane ticket. That was the most peaceful month I had in a long time. There, I got to be a kid again. I felt so protected around Martin. That's where I met Michael, who played the saxophone at church. The first night I went, I found it strange that the church only had about fifteen people, but I figured more would come the following week. I remember sitting in church, staring at Michael. Every time our eyes met, he turned away and smiled. *What an ugly guy; what's wrong with him?* I asked myself. A couple of days later, Michael called the house asking for Martin as if he really needed to speak to him.

So, we ended up talking for over three hours. I felt so special that summer; it had been a while since someone had given me so much attention. I wanted it to last forever. The more we talked, the more I liked him, and the cuter he became in my eyes. All of a sudden, I felt like Georgia was my way out; I wanted to live there. Not just because of Michael, but because I was in a house where no one called me names like "hypocrite." I was always told that I was pretty and smart, and people listened to me. I felt like I was worth something.

The best part of that summer was talking to Michael. The second-best part was going to the beach. I didn't know how to swim, but I still liked the beach, although many people stared at my scar. I always felt free in the water; I felt like I was accepted. I was just another girl in all those people's eyes.

I felt complete during that month, and I didn't want to lose that feeling. Before my trip back to Salem, Martin asked Micho if I could stay with him in Georgia. Micho and Martin had always been friendly, even though Martin was upset at the way Micho had treated my mother.

"No, I like having her here. She cooks for me sometimes," Micho said.

What? I thought. Maybe I didn't hear him correctly, but Micho's actions did not mirror that of someone who liked me. All of a sudden, I was important to him. I couldn't fight it since I was still a minor. I was so sad when it was time for Martin to take me to the airport; it was time to go back to school.

I was terrible at showing emotions. I didn't know how to say I didn't want to go back, so I kept it all inside. I was in line when Martin slipped me forty dollars.

"Thanks," I said. The money meant nothing to me at that time. I just wanted to stay in Georgia. I wanted to scream, "Don't go!" as he walked away, but I didn't know how. I pretended like I was strong, but my heart was breaking into pieces. When I got on the airplane, I sat there, and all I could think of was how miserable I was going to be in Massachusetts. I wanted the years to go by quickly so I could be eighteen and get my own place, but it sounded easier than it really was. I sat there, staring at the window, ready to scream for someone to let me out.

I didn't want the old lady next to me to see how sad I was, so I fixed my eyes on the window. I could not help the tears that ran down my face nonstop. I needed so much for someone to save me, but that wasn't my destiny. I knew Micho loved me, and I knew he wanted me to live with him. I knew he wanted to protect me from this dangerous world, but I don't think he knew how. I don't think he knew how sad we were. He didn't know how much we needed a hug most of the time. I don't think he knew how sick I was of living.

Back in Salem, Sheila had started dating a guy named Evens—a good guy. The kids made fun of him because he carried a briefcase to school, like a lawyer. One day, Sheila came home late, and Micho was watching out the window for her. I guess he saw the guy kiss her. Micho flipped out when she opened the door.

He was a church guy, so that made a little difference to Micho. He assumed if someone was a church member that that person must be good. Evens was clean-cut, dressed well, and he was Haitian. Micho was a very up-front person. He had no filter. Micho demanded that Evens bring his family over to our house for a meeting.

The night, Evens' family visited. Our house looked like we were having an engagement party. Evens' family showed up in a white van from all over Massachusetts. They even brought kids with them. I thought it was funny that the entire family had to come to our house to decide whether or not Sheila and Evens could date. I was in charge of the kids, and I was not allowed in the living room. I hated the fact that I had to care for the kids; I never liked kids. I always wanted to be alone, whether it was watching television, listening to the radio, or reading a book.

Micho was more interested in the guy's character, whether or not he was serious about Sheila. Although I found his actions weird, I thought it was a sign that he cared about what happened to us. Micho later agreed that it was okay for Evens to date Sheila. They could date, but could not go out on a date; I never understood why he made that decision.

"Cynthia, when you're ready to date, we're going to do the same thing," he said.

"I'll never have a boyfriend," I told him. I would never want to have a boyfriend if I had to go through all this drama. What if I realized the day after the meeting that the guy was a jerk? Would we have another family meeting for the breakup? I didn't have time for such nonsense.

Months passed, and I hated my house more each day. Micho laughed with us once in a while, he took us out occasionally, and he even touched our hair when he got home from work sometimes. There were times when we were actually happy living with him, or maybe we made ourselves believe that, but it never lasted. We always had to try harder for those smiles to last. It was hard for us to be ourselves; we always had to pretend to be someone else to win his love. If we were unhappy, we had to pretend to be happy because it was the only way to avoid a lecture on how much we were loved. His "love" was killing us all inside our hearts.

I remember the day of Jephte's wedding. Micho didn't say much to us about the wedding. That afternoon, he wore a gray suit and was getting ready to leave. One of his friends picked him up for the wedding so they could ride together. The man seemed surprised that none of us were dressed up.

"Why are they not going to the wedding?" he asked.

"They are not part of this family anymore," Micho replied.

Not that we cared, since we didn't have any fancy clothes to go to a party anyway. We were actually happy that we weren't invited. If we wanted to be treated like human beings, we had to act like zombies and do whatever we were told to do, even if it meant jumping off a bridge. Two years after we had moved to the United States, Micho continued to choose others over his children.

Right before school started, we had to move again. At that point, I was sixteen years old and entering high school. Normally, a sixteen-year-old would be a junior in high school, but things usually worked a bit differently for immigrants.

"We are moving to the basement," Micho said.

The house was sold, and the new landlord wanted to rent the entire first floor to one family. We did not have a choice because we did not have enough money to help Micho get a better place. It had been a couple years since he applied for Section 8, and he was still on the waiting list, waiting for a two-bedroom apartment to open up. So we simply packed up and brought our stuff downstairs. There was a door that separated the basement from the first floor. In order to get to the basement area, one needed to go in the back of the house. There, we would go down five steps where the basement door was located. There was a small landing. Inside the basement was a full bathroom with a shower on the left side. There was a small kitchenette with a sink and small countertop area on the right side. There was no stove. The landlord provided us with an electric countertop double burner. The kitchenette was located directly next to the entrance.

There were two small windows over the kitchenette area that allowed some sunlight to enter our new home. Right next to the kitchenette was a doorway where two rooms were located. Micho and Paul shared the first room, and Sheila and I shared the second room. In order to get to my room, I had to go through Micho and Paul's room. Sheila and I did not have a door to our room, so Micho used a curtain as a door. The walls were covered with paneling.

Living in that basement brought a certain level of stress because we wondered what would happen if a fire started in the kitchenette. How would we escape? The windows that overlooked the kitchenette area were several feet high and they did not open. Our entire new home was underground except for the doorway.

Our third Christmas in America would be our last inside Micho's home. We all got tired of being together, including Micho. It must have been around six in the morning on a Saturday when he woke us up to tell us that he wanted to see food on the table when he got home that day. He had already stopped shopping for food even though the government gave him food stamps for us. He also wanted each of us to give him one hundred dollars by January 15th or we could all get out. It had already been one year since I had heart surgery. I had never worked, and I didn't have any money to give him. There was no food in the house, so we couldn't cook even if we wanted to; everything was done to punish us.

"What do you expect me to do? Sell my body to put food on the table?" Sheila asked.

Micho hit Sheila on her back with his fist that morning. There was fire in his eyes.

His voice rose as he said, "I don't care what you do, just have food on the table by the time I'm back."

I will never forget the words that came out of his mouth next until the day I go to the grave: "You guys are bitches just like your mother."

I wasn't sure if he said it by accident since he froze afterwards, but it didn't matter; the damage was already done. Those words got to me, and I refused to take any more of his nonsense. I was done, and if it meant I'd have to go to a foster home or sleep under a bridge, then that's what I was going to do. I didn't want to live in that house any longer.

Sheila and I decided to call Martin in Georgia that morning. Her boyfriend, Evens, had purchased a phone card for us to use. We both had tears in our eyes when we spoke to him. We asked if we could come live with him and he accepted.

"You guys will receive the plane tickets by the end of this week," Martin said.

We were saved. We asked Paul to come with us. Martin agreed for Paul to come as well. Although Paul had a different mother and therefore was not related to Martin, he was still welcome to join us in Georgia. Paul didn't want to come along;

he said it wasn't his family. He thought he was strong enough to hang in there.

Now the toughest part was to tell Dad that we were moving to Georgia—or so we thought. We did cook that day, but we didn't eat the food. Evens paid for the food.

When Micho came home that night, both Sheila and I told him we were moving to Georgia the following week. He ate the food we left on the table and never asked who paid for it.

"Good luck in Georgia," he said.

He didn't tell anyone we were leaving. I'm not sure if it was out of embarrassment or spite. But after we left, he said he didn't know we were leaving and that we went because we wanted to take up different men and he wouldn't let us. The night before we left, I called Martin to remind him to pick us up the following day, but he didn't answer, so I decided to call Michael.

"Please tell Martin not to forget to pick me up tomorrow," I told him. I'm not sure why I called him; maybe I wanted him to know that I was coming so he could come to the airport with Martin. Perhaps I wanted to hear his reaction; after all, he did promise the year before that he would drive me around if I ever returned to Atlanta.

It was snowing the morning we were leaving. Evens took us to the airport, and he promised Sheila that he would send her money, and they would always be together no matter what.

My throat got tight when I kissed Micho goodbye. Although he had listened to Nadia and her family for so many years, I could see that he was sad. He looked so helpless that morning, unable to say or do anything. He was so clueless. It was like we'd taken a knife and stabbed him in the heart with it, but the same thing was being done to me, and no one cared. I wanted to believe that I was making a mistake by walking out of his life. Maybe he was right; perhaps I was a hypocrite for not being grateful for what he'd done for me. I wanted to call everything off. I wanted to continue cooking for him even though it was never appreciated. I wanted to be there for him like he was there for me since the day I was born. I tried to tell him that I loved him and that I would come back, but the words "I love you" were not used in my family. There was no way I could spit them out, so I walked out of the door like the hypocrite he thought I was.

On the way to the airport, I thought about my new life and pondered, what if things didn't get better? My mom always told me that sometimes we run from the rain, but we end up in a big river. What if Massachusetts was the rain and Georgia was the big flood? It was a chance that I was going to have to take; I wanted so much to be happy. I would explain everything to Micho one day. He would know that I was worth something one day, but that day wasn't the day. Sheila and I promised to keep in touch with Paul. We were still hoping he would join us in Georgia.

I got on the plane with my cheap teddy bear, which I'd bought years earlier from a garage sale. It was my best friend for a long time, and I wanted to take it with me. The plane was small and only had two rows; it was a scary place to be. I had three choices that day. Go back to my house in Salem, stay on the plane and maybe crash, or still stay on the plane and make it to Georgia. Nothing could be worse than the emptiness inside my heart, so I sat my butt on the plane and held my teddy close to my chest. I felt relieved.

CHAPTER 6

MOVING TO GEORGIA

When we got to Atlanta that Saturday afternoon, we didn't know what to expect. Whatever it was going to be, we knew it was going to be better than Massachusetts.

Martin was single with no children. Martin lived in a two-bedroom apartment. Sheila and I shared one room, and Martin stayed in the other room. Once we got comfortable in our new home, we realized a significant change in our lives. We didn't get a lecture every night anymore. We didn't have to cook every day. When we did cook, no matter what was wrong with the food, we never got a lecture on how stupid and useless we were. Martin still commented on our cooking skills, but it always included a joke. One day I made some bean sauce and it did not taste good at all. The bean sauce was watery and did not taste like Haitian food. Martin joked that I had died right after I made the dish because it was so terrible. Things weren't wonderful like paradise, but they were definitely better than what we were used to. Martin took us shopping; we got to pick a dress for church. About a week later, we registered for school.

Martin, who worked as a local bus driver, took us to school in the morning on his way to work. Sheila was in the middle of twelfth grade and I was in tenth grade. The school was definitely different from what I was used to in Massachusetts. The school in Massachusetts was more segregated. There were several groups in the old school who all stayed separated from each other in cliques. There were whites, Hispanics, African Americans, and the immigrants. I don't think it was done on purpose, but that's just the way it was. Our new school in Atlanta was a bit more diverse. By then, my English had improved, and I started taking a few classes with regular English-speaking students. My classes were also more diverse. My new friends consisted of other Haitians, Asians, Hispanics, and Americans.

My school counselor asked if I wanted to learn how to drive, and I said yes. Mr. Johnson was my driver's education teacher, and he was loud and rude. Although I liked the idea of having a driver's license, I hated that my teacher was so unprofessional. I remember the first day I had to drive; he sat next to me because it was my first time, even though we had student assistants. I sat there, nervous, with my arms shaking.

"Ride your brakes, Ms. Josaphat," he kept yelling. The worst part was when I had to make a right turn. It seemed so hard at the time. Not only did I take forever to turn the car, but I turned in the left lane.

"What the hell are you doing?" he screamed. He really used the "f" word. "You're going to get us killed!" Everyone was riding their brakes; I didn't see how I was going to get us killed.

So he told me to get the hell out of the car and let someone else drive.

Martin made it easy for me to learn how to drive. He taught me how to drive a manual (it wasn't like I had a choice; the only car at the house at the time was manual). First, he drew me instructions on a piece of paper. Up to the left is first gear, below that is second gear, up in the middle is third gear, below that is fourth gear, up on the right is fifth gear, and below that is reverse. It seemed easier than it really was, but it only took me a few minutes to learn how to drive that car. First, we started in the church's parking lot, and then we drove in the streets. I even got to drive home that night.

It was funny how I never missed Massachusetts after moving to Georgia, except for Diana, the girl I'd met in gym class. She was the best friend that anyone could ever ask for. She had her flaws, but her good qualities covered those flaws. Before I left, we promised to write to each other once a week whether we received a letter from each other or not. We also promised to be each other's first child's godmother.

The summer after I moved to Georgia, Diana's parents agreed to let her visit me. I missed the old times; I wanted to see her so badly. Diana and I were like gasoline and matches; whenever we got together, we made a fire. She attended church with us for the entire month that she stayed, and we took the opportunity to bother some people there.

By then, Michael and I weren't talking anymore, but I admired him every week while he played the saxophone. Michael was the perfect guy: tall, light-skinned, muscular, and handsome, with a straight nose, big eyes, and a beautiful smile. The more I attended the church, the more I liked Michael. He was my first true crush. His mother wasn't crazy about me though. I don't think it was anything personal. She just wanted to be the only woman in her son's life. His presence made me nervous because I liked him so much. Going to church became a pleasure and a burden at the same time. I got pleasure from seeing Michael at our weekly church services, but it was a burden not being able to tell him how much I liked him.

I wasn't really sure why Michael's mother didn't like me. She was nice to me when I visited Georgia the summer before. I wasn't the all-Haitian girl who would go to church and kiss church members on their cheeks and ask them how their week went. I wasn't the type to smile whenever my eyes met with someone else's. I didn't have a beautiful enough voice to sing at church. I wasn't part of the church's organizations. My parents didn't have a lot of money; I didn't even live with them. My family didn't drive an expensive car or live in a big house where I had my own room. I didn't wear fancy clothes or go to a beautician every week. No one knew if I would ever be able to go to college. I was anything but the perfect girl.

I remember drinking at the church's water fountain one morning, and I could feel someone next to me. When I was done and ready to leave, Michael was waiting for a drink of water himself.

"Hello, Cynthia," he said.

I got nervous, scared to look at him straight in the eyes, so I ran back inside the church. My heart was pounding, unable to control the feelings I had inside. He thought I ran because I couldn't stand him, but I ran because I liked him too much.

When Michael and I first stopped talking, everyone at church blamed me; I was too rude. He was the perfect kid, the one with a mom and dad. Michael was the kid who played the saxophone at church and sang occasionally. He attended private school and got good grades. Michael smiled when I walked inside the church; he dressed well and waved at anyone whose eyes met with his. He had a car, one given to him by his parents. Everyone saw a future in him, possibly their future doctor or lawyer.

Then there was Pat in my English class, who volunteered to give me a tour of the school when I first moved to Atlanta. Pat had what many of the girls at school wanted a guy to have—a car. That didn't move me, though, as I spent my time comparing him to Michael, externally as well as internally. Pat was shorter than Michael, and he didn't have a cute smile like Michael did. He didn't dress the way Michael did; he wore sneakers and jeans to school. There were times when I wished I liked him; that would've taken my mind off Michael, as I spent most of my days dreaming of Michael. Michael became a drug to me; I couldn't fall asleep without thinking about him and didn't wake up in the morning without thinking about him either. The idea of him was what put a smile on my face most of the time. I dreamed of the day he would give me a hug, the day he would kiss me, and the day he would love me.

And so, I made myself believe that I could like Pat. Maybe if I wanted him, that would take Michael out of my mind, but that didn't help, as he was so interested in sex. While he lived for sex, I lived for someone to love me. The word sex was like a curse to me, something that I never wanted to talk about—I was determined to keep my virginity until marriage. I tried to keep my mind clean, so I prayed three times a day. Maybe if I were good, God would make Michael like me. Perhaps if I remained a virgin, he would learn to love me someday, I thought. And so I made myself believe that, in time, he would want me. I would give him all the time in the world, even if I had to wait forever—something, I realized later, that my mom would've done. Like she'd said, I was going to be just like her and choose the wrong guy in life.

I remember the first time Michael came to church with a girl named Sarah. It was Youth Day. I was in the restroom talking with Diana. We were checking our makeup while Sarah was fixing her long hair. She was so beautiful and voluptuous. I got this weird feeling inside my stomach when I saw them together inside the church; it was as if someone had stabbed me in the heart with a knife. I was so sad and angry that morning. For the first time, a boy had broken my heart. I was embarrassed that I wasn't good enough for him. I wanted to come out of my skin. I tried to get away from the church, but I couldn't. I had to wait for the service to end. I wanted to get up and leave, maybe go hide in the restroom, but that would've been more embarrassing. I had to act like I didn't care, like I never liked him, like he and Sarah didn't matter to me. That day I made a promise to myself that I would never be kind to Michael again. So, together, Diana and I called his house and hung up whenever he said hello just so I could hear his voice. For many years I dreamed of the day Michael was going to like me, unsure if it would come.

I remember once I was a bridesmaid at my friend's wedding and Michael was going to be playing the saxophone. The day before the wedding, a girl walked up to me and said Michael had a crush on me. It must've been my lucky day; this was the guy of my dreams, so I told her it wasn't true.

"He doesn't like me," I told her.

"He's going to try to talk to you tonight," she said.

So I spent the rest of my day thinking about what she said, that she must have been joking. This guy wasn't going to like me in a million years. The next day was the wedding. I had to get dressed at the bride's house, and Michael's mom was the matron of honor. She and I would have to spend the day in the house together, but it wasn't hard, as she ignored me the whole time. It was as if I was not there at all. The night of the wedding was a little scary as I couldn't stop thinking about what the girl had said the day before.

I could not stop staring at him while walking inside the church. We didn't walk with groomsmen, so I had to walk alone. I was the third one of the girls to enter the church, and I could not get myself to stop staring at this amazing person who would never be mine. He smiled when our eyes met, but I didn't. What the hell was I thinking? This was the guy of my dreams.

Then came the reception. I got to sit close to the bride and groom, and Michael sat right across from us. Still, I couldn't stop myself from staring at him. The way he laughed took my breath away. All the girls were getting up to talk to their friends, but I couldn't get up from my seat. I was too embarrassed to walk around in my tight dress. It was around when the cake was served that I decided to go outside for a bit. So he followed me out. I'm not sure why I went outside; maybe I wanted him to follow me.

"I need to talk to you," he said.

"I don't want to talk to you," I said.

He grabbed me by the arm, and we went a few feet away from where the reception was.

"Why don't you talk to me anymore?"

"I don't know."

"What happened?"

"I don't know what happened."

"Where are you going to college?" he asked.

"I'm moving back to Massachusetts."

I wasn't even sure why I said that. I had no plans to move back to Massachusetts. I guess I wanted him to see that I could leave. I wanted him to know that I wasn't going to be around forever and that I could disappear. I am not sure if he knew how much I liked him, but I imagine he had an idea since I was always staring at him and turning away when our eyes met. I imagined if he had fun watching me suffer silently for his attention, then I could end it by going away. The truth was I was madly in love with him and I wanted to be his wife someday.

He kept asking questions that I didn't have answers to. He was the first one who had taken the time to ask me where I was going to college; most people assumed that I wasn't going.

"Maybe we can start over. Would you like us to introduce ourselves like we just met?" he asked.

"Sure," I said.

"My name is Michael," he said. "What's yours?"

I found that to be funny, but I played along. "My name is Cynthia," I said like he didn't already know.

"Forget about the past, and start from the beginning."

"Sure," I agreed, but I didn't mean it. I wanted to, but I didn't think it was possible. I had spent too many months admiring him from a distance, and he had spent too many months ignoring me. We could never start over; it just wasn't worth it anymore. What about his mother? She did not even like me. How would it work? Michael still lived at home. His parents paid for everything he needed. Would he be allowed to date someone they didn't approve of?

That night as we sat in the car and Martin was getting ready to pull away, Michael walked over to the car to say goodbye. "Drive safe, Martin, and goodnight, Cynthia," Michael said. That night I felt like I was floating on clouds. It was magic. His voice was like music to my ears. Could my dreams be coming true? Could Michael actually like me? Only time would tell. I continued to go to church, and Michael continued to play the saxophone, but the night of the wedding was the last time we talked.

CHAPTER 7

MEETING JOHNNY

While living at Martin's house, I met this guy named Johnny, who visited Atlanta for a few weeks from North Carolina. Johnny was visiting with his aunt, who was our next-door neighbor. Johnny's family had moved to the United States from Jamaica when he was a little boy. He became my best male friend, the first guy I thought I was going to spend the rest of my life with after giving up on Michael. Johnny was almost eighteen years old when we met. At nearly eighteen, he was over six feet tall and built, with beautiful eyes. He wore glasses and was very handsome with nice brown skin. By then, I was nineteen years old and had just finished high school.

Johnny and I became very close friends over a three-week period. He had qualities that no one else I knew had. Although Michael had all the qualities a woman would want in a husband, I never really spent enough time with him to benefit from them. Johnny was an excellent listener, and I admired that in him. A couple of days after he got there, I offered to show him around. We could visit the parks and the mall. I asked him what his favorite food was, and he told me rice.

That summer, I spent most of my days hanging out with Johnny. We went to the local park where we carved our names on a large tree that had many other names. It was a symbol that we would remain friends forever. Martin did not seem to have any issues with my friendship with Johnny.

One evening, we were coming from the park, and there was a loose dog in the streets. I used to be so afraid of dogs; it didn't matter if it was a small little puppy. So I told him to stay close to me and not let the dog hurt me, and he held my hand. I couldn't believe he didn't leave me alone that night. He could've run off and left me alone with the dog, but he didn't do that. He held my hand tightly in his, and I felt so safe at that moment. We sat on Martin's car that night, counting stars in the sky. I liked the way he looked at me; it was as if he loved me, and it felt so real. Johnny made it easy to walk away from my feelings for Michael. He made me realize there was much more to life than wasting time on the things I could not have. As amazing as Michael was, he was not good for me. He was what I wanted, not what I needed.

The next day, we went to McDonald's with his little cousin Jerry, who was five years old at the time. Johnny had just received some money from his mom and decided to take me out for fast food. As we stood in line, contemplating what we should buy, Johnny told me to buy whatever I wanted. Carrying Jerry on his back, he told me what he wanted and also said to buy Jerry a kid's meal, right before he handed me a twenty-dollar bill. I noticed an old lady staring at us, smiling. Maybe she thought we were a young couple, and Jerry was our child, so I smiled back. I ordered chicken nuggets, Johnny ordered a Big Mac, and I ordered Jerry a Happy Meal.

I was just sitting there, thinking about life in general, about my future, about Johnny and why he was so lovely to me, about his impending return to North Carolina, he touched my face and said, "Come on, baby, eat." I was just thinking to myself, *Wow, what a sweet line that came out of his mouth.* He took a nugget, dunked it in the barbecue sauce, and put it in my mouth and told me to chew. "I'll be like your mom today," he said, and we both laughed.

I remember crying that night because I felt sad. Someone had called me a terrible person. I sat outside the apartment, and he brought me a big cup of water to drink. "Don't cry," he said. "You're breaking my heart." I could see tears in his eyes. We stayed up as late as we could, just talking. Well, I did most of the talking, and he listened. I told him about Massachusetts, how empty I was inside. I told him how I missed my mom, how I wished she lived with Sheila and me.

My mom and I were still writing letters to one another. Occasionally we spoke over the phone, but that was before the internet was popular and people could communicate freely using apps. Writing letters was fun, but it meant we communicated maybe once a month because mail took longer to be delivered in the States from Haiti.

He listened without question. I had never seen anything like that before, a young man so loving, and I was amazed. The way he wiped my tears, he took my breath away. He decided to give me a foot massage while I had my feet on his lap, and it was my first one ever. Then he massaged my scalp, the one thing that I loved the most in this world. I said to myself, *I think I'm going to marry this guy one day.*

Johnny and I spent nearly a month together while he vacationed with his aunt. I knew he cared a lot about me the day he left for Raleigh. He hugged me, and I gave him my teddy bear. I thought I was never going to see or speak to him again. When it was time for him to leave, I turned to face the window with tears in my eyes; I didn't want him to see me cry. I stared outside the window with tears running down my face as his mom's car pulled away. That night, amazingly, his mom called. He was crying as well, and she wanted me to talk to him to find out what was wrong. "I miss you," he said.

I didn't know what to say. I wanted to tell him I missed him too, but I didn't know how, so I kept it inside. I don't think I'd been that happy in more than four years. Soon after that, he got a job at a fast-food restaurant, bought a phone card every night, and called me. That was before everyone carried a cellphone around. I was always happy when the phone rang and I heard his voice. He was my savior; he always took the heavy weight from my heart when he called. I never understood how he did it. From that day on, we talked for years over the phone. We dated other people, but I knew somewhere deep down that he loved me, and I loved him too, although I never told him.

I remember the first time he told me he loved me; I was shocked. I didn't know what to say, so I didn't say anything. I didn't tell him I'd loved him for almost seven years, but he'd stopped complaining by then.

He told me, "I know you love me, so I won't bug you anymore." I loved him so much but was never able to say the words to him. I was so afraid of loving him; I didn't want another heartbreak, or I didn't want my mother's life. I wanted to make sure he could be trusted before I told him what was in my heart. Johnny was always there for me when I needed him. I couldn't complain. He just did all the things that I never expected a man to do without expecting anything in return.

CHAPTER 8

VISITING MY MOM IN HAITI

The same summer, we found out my mother was sick. At the time, we were not sure what was wrong with her. We thought maybe she had a fever or a cough and that a simple visit to the doctor's office would take care of it. Martin suggested that we take a trip to Haiti to visit my mother.

"You need to visit Haiti to see your mother," he would say time and time again. At first Sheila went and visited. I could not go because my Haitian passport was expired, and I did not have the cash to get a new one right away. After Sheila returned, she agreed that I needed to visit my mom. Her sickness was not that simple. She had pneumonia and she was not getting any better with treatment. Even as doctors continued to treat her and remove fluid from her lungs, she continued to lose weight at a fast pace. Her health continued to decline.

I visited my mom in August of 1997, and she looked horrible. Sheila was able to afford my airline ticket and pocket money since we were not paying for housing when we lived with Martin. When my mom came to pick me up at the airport in Haiti, she looked disfigured—everything about her looks had changed, including her beautiful oriental eyes and dark hair. Her arms were skinny like a one-year-old baby. She must have weighed no more than ninety pounds that day, this woman who used to weigh at least one hundred and forty pounds. I could see her cheekbones stick out. Her skeletal skull could be seen through her skin. She looked shorter than usual. I was afraid of her. It was almost like she'd shrunk. She'd gotten smaller than me, and I never weighed more than one hundred and twenty-three pounds. She was still my mom, though. She hadn't lost her smile, and she could still kill someone with that smile. She was so happy to see me. Don't get me wrong, I was glad to see her also, but I just couldn't keep my eyes on her; it was too painful. I was too scared of her bony body. It was almost like I was looking at a skeleton. I didn't cry; I wanted to, but I just could not. I was known as the tough kid in the family, the strong one who couldn't break; the rough one, without the heart, without the feelings; the one who never laughed nor cried. At least that's what everyone thought.

My emotions were numb, so I didn't cry that day, but I was angry. I was angry at myself because I couldn't help her, mad at Micho for breaking her heart, and furious at nature for letting her be the way she was. It took me two days to look her straight in the eyes. I soon realized that she was the same woman who gave birth to me, the one I adored, my role model.

"Coucou, I missed you so much," she said. That's what she called me. Everyone else called me Cynthia, but that was still the special nickname she gave me. I couldn't say anything; I was speechless, like someone had cut out my tongue and the words that I wanted to say couldn't come out. In that moment, I sat at the table eating, with my hand on the table.

"Cynthia!" my Aunt Claudette said. "You and Nirlande have the same hands."

I looked at her hands and then looked at mine. Indeed, we had the same hands. It was terrific. I liked that idea, having something that she had; that way, I knew I was a part of her. I had her skin complexion and the same hair texture, except my hair was brown, and Mother was much prettier than I was—or so her brothers had told me.

During my visit to Haiti, I got to eat things that I hadn't eaten in years since they were only made there. If they were sold in the States, the taste wasn't the same. I remembered the old days, walking on Champ de Mars from la Ville with a papita (sliced dried plantain, fried with salt) and a fresco (snow cone) in my hands. Spending time with my mom in Haiti made me feel loved again. When crossing the street, she would hold my hand. I remember walking near the State Medical University of Haiti; we were walking to Aunt Claudette's house because that's where I was staying at the time.

The streets of Haiti could be confusing. Drivers rarely obeyed any rules. Very few of the streetlights worked, and there were not many stop or yield signs around the city. Drivers went in and out of lanes to cut in front of other drivers. We had to be very careful while crossing the streets because a hit and run could be deadly with no consequences for the driver. My mom took my hand in hers and proceeded to use her hand to signal the drivers and make eye contact with them, letting them know that she was getting ready to cross.

"Remember, no running while crossing the street," she said to me. I stayed close to my mother while she held my hand. It was the most protected I had felt in a very long time. I followed her lead and took a step whenever she took one. We watched for cars on our left, which was on our side of the street, and walked slowly to the middle, this time paying attention to cars coming in the opposite direction, to our right. It's a very dangerous task but one that many Haitians have mastered over the years. Although I was a big girl now, it still felt good to know that I was protected again. Although she favored Sheila when we lived in Haiti, she was the only person who'd ever loved me unconditionally. I wanted that day to last forever, but I knew it wouldn't.

"There's going to be a picnic at the church," Aunt Claudette said. I was excited to hear that; it would be like old times, when I was a Pathfinder in Haiti. Being a Pathfinder was similar to being a Boy or Girl Scout, except the program is run by the Seventh-day Adventist Church. We went to the supermarket that night and attended the church next to the grocery store. There I saw the director of the Pathfinders, whom I knew from when I was one of them.

"Robert!" I called. He was so happy to see me, and so was everyone else. "I want to go to the picnic," I told him. He pointed to a group of people who wanted to buy tickets, but only two spots were left. He promised to write my name down if I gave him the money right at that moment, which I did.

We sat on the bench at church and talked about old times. Now I had to give him the name of someone I wanted to take with me. Aunt Claudette thought I should take my mom, but I wasn't sure I wanted to; she looked too sick, and part of me was ashamed to be seen with her. I gave my cousin's name, Johanne.

For some reason, my mom thought she was the one going. I didn't know how to tell her that I wasn't taking her. "Let her take Johanne instead, Nirlande," Aunt Claudette said. "They're both young." I could see the disappointment in my mother's eyes, but she smiled and said okay. Aunt Claudette saved me that day.

So, I went to the picnic, and everyone was staring at me as if I were from another planet. Those who remembered me came to say hello, and others who didn't know me either gave me evil looks or ignored me. They thought I was below them because I spoke terrible French, and others thought I was above them because the popular guys were talking to me.

"Ki bò bathroom nan ye?" I asked one of the guys. I wanted to know where the restroom was located.

That morning we got on the bus and made our way to Montrouis to spend the day at the beach. Robert allowed me to borrow his Walkman on the bus so I could listen to music. I could hear some of the girls refer to me as "mop head" because I had box braids—not that I cared because I had my headphones on to block their cruel words. On the beach, people looked at me funny because I could buy luxury things like fresh coconut and Coca-Cola from the glass bottle. I brought lasagna while others brought rice with chicken, typical Haitian dishes. There's nothing wrong with rice and chicken, but I didn't see anything wrong with lasagna either. I had my bathing suit on, although I didn't go in the ocean. I never really learned to swim, so I avoided allowing the ocean to swallow me. I used the well on the beach to bathe. I later changed into regular clothes in someone's shack, which was also on the beach. I was not sure why those people trusted me inside their home when they didn't offer it to anyone else.

Maybe it's true what they say. Those in the diaspora smell and look different from the Haitians living in Haiti. My entire trip to Haiti lasted just about one week. I had a good time in Haiti, but I knew that my mom was going to die soon unless God helped her. I had the feeling, plus the way she looked said it all. We went shopping at "Marché Salomon," an open market near the main cemetery, in the heart of Port-au-Prince. There, I bought ice cream, which my mom paid for. She didn't have a job, but whatever she had, she wanted to spend on me, her daughter. I liked that idea. She was proud to have me as a daughter, and I felt lucky to have her as a mom. In my eyes, she was and would always be the best mom in the entire world.

It was time to return to the States, and Aunt Claudette took me to the airport. My mom came along, but by then, people were no longer allowed on the balcony to see planes take off. People were not even allowed inside the airport without a passport and an airline ticket, so she had to wait outside. I couldn't even count how many times she kissed me that day; she was so sad that I was leaving. I could see her holding her tears back as her voice changed tone. I don't know why, but I didn't feel very sad that day, just angry that I couldn't take her with me.

"Coucou, I'm going to stay right here waiting for you," she said. "I will not leave until you come out, even if I wait the whole night." She wanted me to go inside the airport to check-in and then return to spend some more time with her before take-off. I didn't want her to hurt more; I thought she would get over it quicker if she didn't see me. In my mind, one last hug or kiss would hurt her even more, so I decided not to go back outside. She made me promise to go back, and I promised, but I didn't keep that promise. If only I knew, I would've done things differently.

I got some tears in my eyes while standing in line to check my luggage; I waited for two hours before the plane took off, and all that time, she was outside waiting for me, her baby girl, and I let her down. She had never done such a thing to me in my entire life. I betrayed her. At that moment, I became the hypocrite that everyone said I was. I hurt the only woman who ever loved me unconditionally. She never complained about it, though; she forgave me because she loved me. It was the biggest mistake I had ever made in my life and one that I spent years trying to forgive myself for.

CHAPTER 9:

DEPRESSION

Sheila and I moved out of Martin's place in the fall of 1997, just a few months after Johnny left. We'd lived with Martin for almost three years, but after both of us finished high school and Sheila started attending a local community college part-time, it was time to spread our own wings. Sheila was able to get financial aid to pay for the tuition. I was grateful to Martin for caring for us during those years, a job he had claimed when he didn't have to, and he had done his best to provide us with a home. I temporarily moved back to Massachusetts with my best friend Diana, and Sheila moved into a small efficiency apartment that she rented about ten minutes from Martin's house.

Once Sheila settled there, I moved back to Atlanta and started going to a technical school where I studied to become a Medical Secretary.

Our new efficiency apartment was small but cozy. It was situated in the back of another family home so no one could see it unless that person entered the yard. The efficiency had a small bathroom, enough room for a sofa, a medium-sized fridge, and a small kitchenette. There was a door to our bedroom, which provided us with some privacy. The entire unit measured no more than two hundred square feet.

It would take around nine months for me to receive my Medical Secretary certificate. The program would cost around ten thousand dollars from start to finish. I did not have any money, of course, so I met with a counselor to discuss payment options. During the meeting, the counselor asked me to complete the Free Application for Federal Student Aid (FAFSA). I had to provide information related to my citizenship status and family income, which was zero in my case, since I was not working and I did not live with either of my parents. The purpose of the application was for the school to determine how much money I could afford to pay for school based on my household income. Due to my age, I needed to provide my parents' income tax return, which I did not have. At last, I was allowed to submit affidavits from close family and friends certifying that my mother lived in Haiti and my father was not a part of my life. Because I was living below the poverty line, I was eligible for the full grant amount plus student loans. I was also asked to pay around thirty-five dollars a month in fees to the school.

Georgia was a tough place to try to find work back then. I don't know if the problem was the stores or me, but no place wanted to hire me; it was just so hard to get a job. Almost every day I woke up and walked to a new store to fill out an application. I had hoped to get a job at a local supermarket located just a couple blocks from my house. It would have been easy to get to work since neither Sheila nor I owned a car. I applied for work at nearly every single store or restaurant I could walk to, but not one of them called me. I even applied to work at a Haitian restaurant, where I did, in fact, get hired, but the pay was only fifteen dollars for a full day of work. I only held that job for one day and decided it wasn't worth it. It wasn't even legal pay.

For months, Sheila and I lived on a job she had at Kentucky Fried Chicken (KFC), where she made no more than seven hundred dollars a month. We used that money for food, rent, transportation, and bought clothes whenever possible. We also sent money to my mom in Haiti.

It's incredible the things we can do when we don't have a choice. I was the cook in the house, and I bought fifty dollars worth of groceries every month. That food lasted us the entire month, and we never went hungry. The fridge was never empty. Although there wasn't anyone to give us headaches in the house, my life was so empty. Of course, I couldn't tell anyone except for Johnny, but he wasn't around in person. All our conversations were over the telephone. I also had my friend Diana's support, but she was pregnant with my goddaughter at the time. She had her own crap to deal with, and I couldn't bring my problems into her life. It seemed as if everything happened at the same time: Diana getting pregnant; Johnny going away and not doing so well with his personal life, but remaining supportive of me; me not having a job; and my mom being sick. I felt a big cloud over my head and a heavy weight squeezing my heart. I was going out of my mind, and I wanted to wake up from this terrible nightmare—but it wasn't a dream, this was reality. I couldn't run away from it; this was my life.

I hated who I was. There wasn't anything good about me, and soon I was too rude for the people at the church. People started judging me. I wasn't classy enough; I wasn't the sweet girl that everyone expected me to be; I didn't smile enough; I wasn't submissive enough. Some of it was true, but most of it was untrue. Some people even thought I was sleeping around with guys because I would wear pants to church, painted my nails blue, and took advice from no one. The way I saw it, if you didn't know anything about my life, how could you tell me how to live it? Everyone seemed against me. I needed to make the best of the situation, and anyone who couldn't understand it my way had to go to hell. The worst part was that I started to hate myself—the fact that I was ever born.

I hadn't spoken to Micho since I'd moved to Georgia. My mom was sick, and we wrote to one another, but she couldn't help me. In fact, she needed my help, and I was in no position to help her. We knew my mom had pneumonia and a family doctor was removing fluid from her lungs several times a week, but other people started to question whether her sickness was related to voodoo because that was the reason given when a medical doctor was unable to treat a patient's illness. My life was empty. I felt constant pain in my stomach, and I started to cry for no reason. I began to read more books about sadness until I got to the books written about depression. That was it: I was depressed. I started to read the whole night through, slept the next morning, and did it all over again. The only thing that kept me going was talking to Johnny, but I couldn't do it twenty-four hours a day.

He lived several hours away. I didn't have a job, and he no longer had one either, so we couldn't see one another. I remember sitting on our couch one night, and I was just angry. I wanted to punch a hole in the wall, but that was not my style. I considered suicide—life just wasn't worth living anymore. If I had to live such an empty life, then I'd rather be dead. I didn't care about the ones I was leaving behind; no one cared about me anyway. The reason why I was empty in the first place was that there wasn't anyone around. No one would cry for me after I was gone, except for my mom. She was the only one who seemed to care, although she was in no position to help me. The way I saw it, she would get over it. Death is a part of life. We can't get used to it, but we surely get over it with time.

I wanted to get rid of the feeling I had inside; it was almost like someone took a hammer and smashed my heart. My chest was so tight that it felt like I was having a heart attack, but that wasn't the case. I felt angry, sad, and hopeless all at the same time. That night, I walked over to the bathroom and I looked at myself in the mirror. I hated what I saw. My eyes were red, tears kept flowing out of my eyes, and I looked sad. I hit my right arm against the bathroom wall. It hurt but felt good at the same time. So I hit it again, and again, and again. The more I did it, the better I felt. Soon the cloud that was over my head was gone, the hammer stopped smashing my heart, and I didn't feel like crying anymore, but I did have a swollen wrist.

I walked over to the local hospital, which was located a few blocks from my house. It was a safe place; the doctors and nurses would care about me.

"What happened?" the doctor asked.

"I fell," I responded.

That was a complete lie, but I couldn't tell them the truth. They would have called the mental health office and have me involuntarily committed. A trip to the local hospital was my only option when it came to seeing a doctor since I didn't have health insurance. I don't think the hospitals were allowed to turn me away even if I could not pay.

"It's not broken," the doctor said in the emergency room after looking at the x-ray.

They put a bandage around my wrist and gave me a sling to support my arm that went around my neck. The doctor suggested I take Tylenol for pain. Neither the doctors nor the nurses questioned my story about falling and hurting my wrist. I was a non-paying patient. They only needed to do the bare minimum and send me on my way. The hospital bills came and went, but nothing came of them because I could not pay, and I was not eligible for Medicaid because I was no longer a minor. I didn't need Tylenol; it didn't hurt. I was too numb inside, and I felt nothing physically or emotionally. I kept that thing on for no more than a week; my wrist was soon the way it was before I hit it on the wall. After that incident, I promised myself that I'd never do that again—at least not to make my pain go away. I was feeling better, but I should've known better. The first time I'd taken those pills, years before, I'd set myself up for something that I wouldn't be able to get rid of easily.

I was still going to school and I was actually doing okay. I attended school for around four hours a day between the hours of 8 a.m. and 12 p.m. I caught the public bus one block from my house and transferred to another bus half-way to school. The school was actually located in a different city, so I had to catch a second bus once I got to the second city to take me to school. The entire ride lasted nearly an hour on some days, depending on traffic. My favorite subject was anatomy, even though I had never been good at subjects related to science, which was surprising to me. No matter how bad I felt, I still woke up and went to school because I knew it was my only way out of poverty.

Dealing with depression was much harder for me as a Haitian because the word was almost nonexistent in my community. Being depressed meant a weakness. What would other people think if they knew I was sick in my mind? What would they say? Would they call me crazy? I had never met a Haitian who believed mental illness was a true sickness. Anyone who didn't have it together one hundred percent was called "moun fou," meaning crazy person. I was not crazy, so I did not want to be called that. Being Haitian made it so much harder to get the help that I desperately needed because there was such a shame attached to mental illness. I could not tell my family what I was feeling because they would not care; they would not care because they could not understand it. Johnny understood, but he was young himself and could only lend me his ears to vent. People would tell me to pray harder, stop thinking about the negative, and focus on the positive. They would tell me that it was all in my head. But the pain was real. The sadness was real. The knot in my stomach was real. The tears were real. The hopelessness was real. The feeling of not wanting to be alive for another minute was overwhelming and very real.

Where would I find the money to see a therapist? My sister made about $700 a month for the two of us to live on. We had to pay for rent, groceries, toiletries, and bus passes. I had no health insurance and I could not afford it either. At that point, I had no idea what was going on with my heart because I could not afford to see a cardiologist either. I was in survival mode.

It had been more than three years since we'd moved to Georgia, and my mom was getting worse. Months passed, and she continued to get worse; she was dying. I started to have dreams about black dresses, me in a casket, funerals, cemeteries, stuff like that. It was scaring me, but I couldn't stop them, they were my dreams, and I had to face them.

CHAPTER 10:

LOSING MY MOM

I received a phone call from Haiti on May 15, 1998, close to midnight; it was Uncle Anel's wife from Haiti. I got scared before I even knew what was wrong.

"Cynthia!" my Uncle Anel's wife said. "I don't think your mom is going to last the night." I dropped to the floor, and I got that feeling in my stomach once again. I couldn't help the tears that were running down my face. The next day was my birthday; I didn't want my mother to die on my birthday.

"No," I told my aunt, "not on my birthday."

When Sheila saw me sitting on the kitchen floor speechless, with the phone in my hand, she thought my mom had died, and she screamed.

"She's not dead," I said, "but she's close."

We were so alone, with little money; I didn't even have a bank account. Sheila still had the job where she made seven hundred dollars a month for the both of us. How were we going to bury our mother? We didn't have any money; how would we go to Haiti? We had to take an airplane if she died. I wanted to see her alive, but where would I get the money to pay for the ticket? How would I react when I see her? She probably weighed no more than sixty pounds by then; it was killing me.

I often talked to Diana and Johnny. They were the only support that I had, but they couldn't help me. No one could. I was like a bomb waiting to explode, and once it did, there was no turning back. My heart hardened like a stone; nothing could get inside of it. I had been alone for too long. I didn't need affection anymore, so I stopped caring about people altogether. I didn't want my mom to die, but she was suffering. I wanted her to get better and be happy, or die. I loved her so much, but I did not tell her much except for when I wrote her letters.

People said my heart was tough because of how I handled the situation. I acted as if I wasn't feeling anything at all, but I was just dying inside. Two months passed, and my mom was still alive, but I got the news that she was suffering around the clock. I couldn't even imagine what she was going through during that time. She must have been miserable, and I wasn't there to hold her hand and tell her that things were going to be okay. Doctors said my mother had pneumonia, but neighbors said it was voodoo.

About three months after getting that call from Uncle Anel's wife, I was walking to the bus stop one morning. The bus stop was located one block from my house. I noticed a lady walking in front of me. She reminded me so much of my mother, she scared me a bit. By the time I got to the bus stop, she was already across the street, staring at me like she knew me. I took the bus and went to school. When I got to school, I was still bothered by the lady I had seen earlier. There, I confided in a classmate that I had seen a lady who reminded me so much of my mother that it scared me. My friend and classmate told me it was a sign my mom was dying and that she'd come to visit me in spirit. She suggested that I hurry up and hire a voodoo priest in an attempt to save her life. But I could never do that because I was raised to rely on God for all my needs and wants, and if voodoo was going to save my mother that day, then I'd rather her be dead in Jesus than alive through voodoo.

At precisely six that evening, I got a phone call from Martin. "Call Haiti," he said.

I told him I wanted him to tell me what was wrong. I didn't want to call Haiti unless someone told me what was going on.

"Is my mom dead?" I asked.

"Yes," he replied.

"Okay," I said.

My mother took her last breath on August 14, 1998. I felt nothing that day. I was numb inside, and my heart was like a rock that nothing could get through. I didn't know what to feel or do; I didn't know if I was mad or sad. All of a sudden, Micho came to my mind. He broke my mother's heart and never even took the time to say sorry. He never talked to her until the day she died. I remember not knowing how to tell Sheila since she was always so jumpy, so I asked her best friend, Sissy, to tell her that our mother had died. She acted the same way I expected her to. She cried so hard that I got even angrier. I knew she was hurting, but I was hurting too. The thing was, one of us had to be strong. I had to think quickly. We had no money for the funeral or a plane ticket.

That evening, several people from the church visited to offer their condolences. One by one, they prayed with us and asked God to give us the strength to move forward with life. Each time someone knocked on the door, I jumped. I became terrified of sounds. I was sad and angry. Some people brought us black coffee, no sugar or milk. "It will help with the shock," the ladies said. Others brought tea. Everyone reassured us that things would be okay; we needed to trust in God. But I wasn't ready for their advice. At just around twenty years old, I had just lost the only human being who had ever loved me unconditionally, but no one understood.

How dare she leave me like this, without saying goodbye? I didn't cry the day my mother died. I had too many questions that needed to be answered. Why did she die so young? Was she really dead? Did she do anything that could have caused her death? Could I have done anything to prevent her death? How much did she suffer? What would my life look like without her in it?

All of a sudden, I was not hungry. I had a headache, I was sad, angry, numb, cold, hot, all at that same time. It felt like a dream, a nightmare. A nightmare I would never wake up from.

The day my mother died, my friend Joey visited and asked if I wanted to take a walk. My emotions were all over the place, so I said yes. As we walked, he asked how I was doing. How was I doing? That was a good question; I had no idea how I was doing. I was too numb to answer that question. "I am angry," I said. Joey and I must have walked for over an hour, and I told him stories about my mother. Like when I used to ask her to carry me in Haiti and she would say my legs were too long. Or when she would have an outfit made for herself and she would have a similar one made for me.

Joey told me that my heart was either going to get softer or colder, and he was somewhat right, my heart got cold … and soft. Soft, because I cried when others hurt; I was always ready to help anyone in trouble because I knew how it felt to need help and not get it. My heart got colder because I was quick to walk away from anything that hurt or stressed me; I could walk away from anyone and feel absolutely nothing, as if the person never existed. Diana later told me that a human being wasn't supposed to have a heart this cold, but she didn't understand. It had been a prolonged, painful process—it didn't happen overnight. I was like a bomb waiting to explode, and I guess I did explode. It was going to take more than a year or two to put my heart back together.

Micho called at five in the morning the next day. He said my Aunt Claudette had called him; he wanted to give us his condolences. Condolences? My mother was legally his wife. As far as the law was concerned, they were still married. They were not divorced.

"We don't have any money. Please give one of us a plane ticket for the funeral," Sheila said.

"I don't have any money. I'm getting married to Nadia in a few months," he said.

I told Sheila to hang up the phone because I felt like we could use that time to sleep and figure out what we were going to do that morning. Some of Micho's relatives called and apologized, but that didn't change anything; it didn't help the situation. Sheila and I were given, all together, $150 by Micho's relatives to help with the funeral. Micho didn't contribute anything. It wasn't about money; money could not make it better. Each ticket cost $300, plus the funeral was about $3,000. My sister's friend, Sissy, paid for her airline ticket, and one of my sister's male friends paid for my airline ticket. A lady at the church gave us $40 each for pocket money.

We got to Haiti on Thursday afternoon, and the funeral was scheduled for the next day. It felt funny not having Mom there in person. I don't know if it was because I was going crazy, but I thought she was still alive somewhere in my mind. It felt weird not having her there waiting for me at the airport. I almost expected to see her, even if no one else did. I wanted her to be there for me, maybe to say goodbye since I missed the last opportunity.

My cousin, Johanne, who was still living in Haiti at the time, told me how much my mother suffered before she died. After we left Haiti, and Micho stopped communicating with my mom, one of my mom's siblings asked her to move out of my grandfather's house because she could not afford to pay the $300 rent fee per year. The house was then rented to Uncle Anel and his family, and my mom was forced to live with them. After my mom started to get sick, Aunt Claudette moved her to one of my grandmother's houses which was sitting empty. There, my mom lived in peace by herself, except she was getting too weak to care for herself.

So, Johanne helped her with her baths and meals. As my mom got worse without a caretaker, and Aunt Claudette lived across town fifteen minutes away by car, my mother was sometimes left to sleep in her urine and feces. At times, Johanne told me she would sneak in there to care for my mom without anyone knowing. Johanne told me stories of being unable to fall asleep in the middle of the night from the sound of my mother groaning. My late grandfather's house and my grandmother's houses shared a wall. Aunt Claudette finally made the decision to move my mother to the hospital where she ultimately succumbed to her illness.

Aunt Claudette paid a family friend to stay with my mother at the hospital. The lady was a good friend of my grandmother, so she had watched my mother grow up as a child. A few days before my mother died, the lady told Aunt Claudette, "Someone came to get your patient last night." That was the term used when someone was cursed with voodoo and about to die. Aunt Claudette drove home, and halfway between her driveway and her house, she dropped to her knees and screamed for Jesus. She cried uncontrollably on her knees with her hands up in the air, begging God for mercy. She wished she had called the pastor earlier and asked for prayers. My mother died soon after.

The next day was the funeral. "It's at seven in the morning," Aunt Claudette said. Everyone was nervous, especially Sheila and me. We were the only two children she had. Paul was still living in Salem, and he couldn't come to the funeral. Although we still talked to him, we had not seen him since we left Salem for Atlanta. When we got to the church that morning, it seemed weird that I was going to my mom's funeral. It felt like a prank. The whole thing felt like a dream. My heart started to beat fast when the hearse came with the casket. I couldn't believe that my mom was going to be in the same room with us, but unable to walk and talk.

When the hearse showed up, it became a little more real. At first, a white hearse came, and it was covered with mud. This infuriated Aunt Claudette because this was not the funeral home she would have chosen for my mother. The day my mom died, Aunt Claudette had contacted Pax Villa to pick up the body, but it was too late. Someone had already authorized a local funeral home to pick her up. Pax Villa was a more reputable funeral home in Haiti. Back then, funeral homes used to pay a referral fee of ten percent from the funeral cost. This used to lead to a lot of headaches for families since people with no legal authority were referring bodies in order to receive a portion of the funeral costs. Families who wanted to move their loved ones' bodies were forced to pay a fee to the current funeral home or get law enforcement involved which was time consuming and costly. The local funeral home that handled my mother's body was located near the main cemetery in a run-down building that was not even equipped with a good generator. Aunt Claudette was visibly upset at the sight of this muddy, covered hearse and ordered the driver to leave and return with a clean one. Within a few minutes, a black hearse showed up with my mother, and a few men gathered and carried her inside the church, where we would have a viewing for one hour before the service started.

I felt a big cloud over my head. I felt nothing but anger that morning; not one teardrop came from my eyes. Although it's part of my culture for people to kiss family members who sit in the front row at a funeral, I didn't receive a kiss from anyone, not even the people that I knew. I did not know who I could trust. At that point, I didn't trust anyone because there were so many doubts around how my mother had died. I had an idea of how she died, but I didn't know the exact story. I knew she had pneumonia and a doctor had been removing fluid from her lungs with a needle. I knew she lost a huge amount of weight and continued to deteriorate. I knew there were speculations that she had been cursed with voodoo. One neighbor even pulled me aside and told me who killed my mother. Before my mother died, neighbors reported that she would sit in front of her house and talk to herself. At one point, someone asked her who she was talking to, and she said a man had come to pick up a suitcase he had asked her to hold for him earlier. The only problem was the person had been dead for a few years and my mom didn't seem to recognize that. I didn't know what to believe anymore, so my superstitions kicked in naturally. No one was allowed to kiss me at the funeral in case the rumors were true.

Sheila and Johanne, whom my mom raised when she was a little girl, were out of control in front of the casket. They screamed their lungs out.

"Mom, please wake up," Sheila kept saying. "I'm here, get up for me, please."

My mother didn't wake up, of course. She was dead, and she was never coming back. The casket was opened for less than an hour before Aunt Claudette asked the pastor to close it because the body was releasing a dreadful smell that invaded the entire church. I never got up once to look at my mother's face. I sat close to the door on the left side of the church and stared at the street the entire time. I didn't want to see her face; I didn't want to remember her that way. I didn't want her death to become a reality.

Sheila later told me that her face and neck were swollen and dark. My mom was a light-skinned woman. She died right after she ate a stew at the hospital. My mom died at noon the day we got the call. I'd always been fearful of caskets, and the fact that she was my mom didn't make things any easier. It was Hell when it was time to close the casket. Everyone went one last time to see her face, and each one of those people had tears in their eyes when they walked away. I wanted the whole thing to be a misunderstanding. I wanted her to be alive.

My mom's funeral service was beautiful. I didn't know the pastor because I had not attended that church in Haiti in about six years. That's how many years had passed between the time I moved to the United States and the time my mother died. Six years. A lady who performed a special song wore the same dress as the corpse. At one point, I looked at Aunt Claudette and she blinked at me as a way to tell me not to laugh. Other people had funny looks on their faces. We didn't see the lady again after she performed the song.

The pastor preached a beautiful sermon. He told a beautiful story about my mother's life; he didn't even know her. He described a woman who was God-fearing and someone who had a husband and children. According to the pastor, my mother had left a husband and two children behind. If only he had taken the time to know my mother when she was alive, he would have known that she was only a wife on paper, but the man she loved never loved her back. He would have known her suffering, her lonely days, what she went through while she was sick. How she lost her children in the hope that they would have a better life in a foreign country. The pastor assured us that we would see my mother again because she had died in Jesus and one day, she would rise again in the second coming and we would live forever in Heaven. Heaven couldn't come any sooner for me because I needed my mom right then and there.

On our way to the cemetery, some kids sang a song of farewell. It was so sad that I wanted to cry, but I didn't. I was too angry to cry. We walked behind the hearse; the church was only three blocks from the cemetery. Almost everyone did it at every funeral. There was no limousine to drive us there. I stared at the casket as I walked beside my cousin, Robin. He tried to hide it, but his eyes were red. He and my mom had gotten close before she died. Once we got to the cemetery, the hearse drove as far as it could before stopping. Martin and Uncle Anel helped carry the casket to the grave. My mom's final resting place was a four-person above-ground tomb. It was huge. In fact, most of the graves in that cemetery were big. Very few people, if any, were buried under the ground. My mom's family paid for the funeral. Micho did not give one cent and did not send one card or flowers.

When we got close to the tomb, it was like my mom knew she was going to be placed in the tomb, and she didn't want to go there. The casket got heavy and fell halfway to the ground; I felt that one in my heart. She didn't want to go because she didn't want to leave us behind. She loved us too much. She was placed in the tomb, because, as a dead woman, she had no say. The pastor prayed over the casket and threw some dust on it.

"Souviens toi que tu es poussière et tu retourneras dans la poussière," he said. "Remember, you're dust, and to dust you will return."

"Nanette!" my childhood friend, Maude, screamed in the cemetery. That's what she called Mom. "Who's going to feed me when I'm hungry, now that you're not here?"

That hurt even more, and for the first time since my mom died, I couldn't help the tears that were running down my face. Out of the blue, my chest got tight, my throat was filling up, and

I started shaking. It wasn't supposed to happen this way; she was supposed to live to visit other countries, maybe France or Israel. My maternal grandfather held French citizenship, which he acquired from birth from his own father. Although my grandfather didn't pass down French citizenship to any of his children, I knew my mother had always wanted to visit Paris, specifically *Les Champs Elysees*. We had seen pictures of it on television from French movies and music videos for years. Easter was always her favorite holiday because Haitian television stations always played the *La Vie de Jesus* movie about the Life of Jesus.

I wanted her to grow old to see her grandchildren; I wanted to give her the life that she never had. I wanted to pay her back for everything she had done for me.

How can someone be born unhappy and die unhappy? I still don't understand why things happened the way they did. My mother died in her late forties. She was supposed to live to be ninety or older, to be a beautiful old woman. I had it all planned out. She wasn't going to live in a nursing home. I was going to take care of her myself, give her nothing but the best, and maybe build her a mansion in Haiti. She could have remarried a man who loved her. I wanted her to have a life; she deserved it, and so much more.

Aunt Claudette had gotten a wreath done for her tomb. It read, "Sheila and Cynthia." It was too bad my mother would never be able to see it, not in this lifetime.

Well, we left her there. Although she loved and gave a lot to people, she went by herself. I wanted to get the whole thing out of my head, so I went shopping that day. In a way, I was happy that she wasn't suffering anymore; she was at peace now. I thought life would continue, and I would surely see her in

Heaven one day. It was time for me to go on, have the life that she wanted me to have, be a good person in society, and never let go of the one thing that she gave me—God's word. I promised myself never to let go of that. I didn't want to let her down, and I surely wanted to see her again, so I promised myself to live a righteous life and follow God's laws for as long as I live. At least that's what I wanted to do. The time those teardrops came out at the funeral was the only time I'd cried since she had died; I thought I was strong. That was until reality hit. Nothing in life prepared me for life without my mother.

CHAPTER 11:

LIFE WITHOUT MY MOM

After returning to Atlanta, I had this crazy idea that my mom was still alive. I'm not sure where I got the idea from. Someone could have made a mistake; maybe it wasn't her in the casket. After all, I didn't see her face, so I had no proof that it was her. For weeks, I went to the mailbox every day, looking for a letter from her. The letter never came because she wasn't alive; she could not write any letters to me ever again. How could one person have suffered so much throughout her life? How could life have been so unfair? I was going through my mom's stuff one night at my house when I saw her marriage certificate. Something caught my attention. My mom was buried on Micho's birthday, what a coincidence. The more I waited for her letter, the more paranoid I became. I got scared of her being around me; I even got scared when I heard her name. Soon I started having nightmares about her trying to tell me something in my dreams; I never listened, though—I was always too scared.

In one dream, I was walking in my yard in Haiti toward the street, and once I reached my grandmother's house, my mother would jump out in front of me from under the stairs. Even in my dreams, I knew my mother was dead and I did not want to talk to her. It was the devil dressing up like her, I kept telling myself. In another dream, she was chasing me outside the efficiency and I jumped through the window to get away from her and she jumped in right behind me. Each time, I would jump up from my dreams covered in sweat, scared. The dreams became more frequent over time.

I decided to stop wearing black, although, in Haitian culture, I was supposed to wear plain black for two consecutive years. That's the number of years given to grieve for mothers. It's one year for fathers. But I didn't see it that way. I started wearing all kinds of colors, especially red, to make those dreams go away. It worked. I had heard of stories where the color red scared ghosts, which is exactly what my mother had become, a ghost. I stopped dreaming about her as soon as I stopped wearing black. Soon after, Sheila started having the same dreams. Her dreams seemed to be identical to mine. My mother started chasing Sheila in her dreams, so soon, Sheila stopped wearing black too, and the dreams stopped.

As I grieved for my mother, I continued to attend technical school so I could get my certificate as a Medical Secretary. When I was not studying, I was reading a book on how to deal with loss. Other times, I hid inside the efficiency and begged God for mercy. At one point, I called a psychic hotline; the first few minutes were free. I wanted the psychic to tell me what was going to happen in my future because I hated the waiting game.

"Where's your family?" she asked. "You're all alone," she said. Unfortunately, she had nothing else to offer me. My days were filled with school, studying, and reading. I read every book I could find on depression and loss. The more I read, the more delusional I became. One night, I lay on the sofa staring at the ceiling. It must have been around 1 a.m., and I could actually see images on the ceiling. One night the pain was so overwhelming that I ran to the bathroom to cry. I looked in the mirror and I could see my mother's face staring back at me. I was going out of my mind.

My sleep pattern was unhealthy as I spent big chunks of my nights reading, afraid to close my eyes so I would not see her. I continued to talk to Johnny whenever I could, but it was not every day. My sister had no clue what I was going through. I could not tell her. She was grieving in her own way. I mostly kept my pain to myself.

At first, I didn't miss Mom that much. I thought I was going to see her again; she had to be alive. I knew she had died. I went to her funeral and I was there when my uncles placed her casket inside the tomb. I refused to talk to her in my dreams because I saw her as a ghost, and yet, a part of me still wanted her to be alive. I am not sure what I would have done if I had received a letter in the mail with my mother's name and handwriting. I imagined I would have probably answered it and kept it to myself. I would probably make myself believe that I was right, she was alive after all, and she and I could continue our relationship through letters with no one knowing the truth.

I got tired of being me; I wanted to do something stupid, which was against what was right. I had done everything by the book all those years, and one bad thing was happening after another. I wanted to break the cycle and just be bad for once in my life. I thought of everything, and the only thing I could come up with was to have a man. I had tried very hard to be a good Christian. I had always believed in the power of prayer, and here I was, alone without the one human being who ever loved me unconditionally. Where was God? Was He even real? Why did He let this happen if He loved me? Should I keep serving a God who allowed all those things to happen to my mother and to me? All those questions were racing through my mind. Should I still live a life that is pleasing to the Lord? Does it even matter? Is Heaven real? Is Hell real? Where do I go from here? There was complete darkness every way I turned.

I needed someone to hold me and hug me. It had been six years since my mom held me inside her home before I moved to the United States, and one year since she held my hand while I visited her in Haiti. No one had held me since then. I needed someone to tell me that things were going to be okay, that I wasn't the bad person everyone thought I was.

Everything I did, I did to fill that hole in my heart, and yet the hole got deeper every day. I fell deeper into depression when I finally accepted the fact that my mom wasn't coming back. I was empty because she was missing from my life, and I didn't know how to fix that. She was never coming back. I still don't respect the two-year grieving period given in the Haitian culture, because years later, I was still grieving, and the more time passed by, the more it hurt.

I started to read more about depression and how to cope with losing someone. I thought I was going crazy; I wanted nothing more than to die and never see light again. How could life have been so unfair? Why did she have to die? Those were the questions I asked myself for days, weeks, months, and years. Why was my mom taken away from me so early? I was only twenty years old when my mother died.

My relationship with Sheila started to change. She started to spend more time at her friend's house. We talked less. We cared less about each other, and slowly we started falling apart and becoming strangers. A few months after my mom died, I graduated from technical school and started looking for work in a doctor's office.

A few months after my mother's death, Sheila and I split. "The only thing that kept us together is gone. Since Mom doesn't exist anymore, nothing's holding us together," Sheila said to me.

Maybe she was depressed just like I was, but she never talked about it. I didn't care to hear about it, either. The way I saw it, I could make it without her. The only difference was she had her best friend to go to, and I had nobody. The efficiency apartment was under her name so I couldn't live there anymore. I had nowhere to go.

CHAPTER 12

LIFE BY MYSELF

I had just started a job at the airport as a scanner. At the time, I was still looking for a job in a doctor's office. I worked as part of a team that scanned people's luggage and people's bodies before they were allowed to enter the boarding area. Nowadays, that job is done by the Transportation Services Administration. I used to work at night, so it wasn't so bad because I didn't sleep nights anyway, but I needed a place to sleep during the day. I had no money to get a place. I asked Paul for help, but he didn't have any money either. He promised to help, though, as soon as he could.

For days, I found myself sitting at the bus stop, thinking about where I was going to lay my head. Some days I could barely keep my eyes open. I used to sit there to pass the time, but other times I would stay on the bus just to get some sleep. This went on for at least a couple weeks.

I found a studio apartment for $250 a month in the ghetto, but I didn't have the money to pay to move in. The landlord promised to hold it for me until I received my first paycheck. I met a friend at work named Maria, who sometimes cooked for me and brought the food to work. She also used to let me get some sleep at her house, but I couldn't do that a lot because she lived with her sister. It was January 1st, Haitian Independence Day. I still didn't have enough money to pay for my studio; I had until the fifteenth to move in.

I went to Martin's house to visit for the New Year and to have some pumpkin soup; it's a tradition that Haitians eat pumpkin soup each January 1st to celebrate their independence from the French. I couldn't stay up; I fell asleep on the table, and Martin asked me to get some sleep in one of the rooms. After I'd slept for nearly twelve hours, Martin told me I could stay there for as long as I needed. I am not really sure what made him think I had no place to live other than the fact that I'd fallen asleep at his table. For the next week or so, I slept at Martin's house until I had enough money to move into the studio.

Other than Maria, my coworkers did not know what I was going through because I didn't tell anyone. I didn't even tell Paul or Diana. Johnny had no idea either. It was too embarrassing and too painful to discuss. Sheila and I had zero contact by then, so it was not any of her business anyway. By then, I had stopped going to church completely, so no one from the church knew what was happening with me. There were not many people left in my life. I had not had contact with Micho in years and I did not speak with any of his relatives. I had no contact with Nadia's kids, and I had no time to tell anyone in Haiti the drama that was unfolding in my life. Everyone was busy trying to take care of their own lives. No one had time for me or my issues. I figured if they cared, they would've known.

Right after I moved into the studio, maybe a week later, I lost my job at the airport. The contract had ended, and I was dead broke with no help. I needed to intensify my job search and find something in a doctor's office, but the search was more challenging than I originally thought.

Something was still wrong; I was so empty inside. I needed something to fill that hole in my heart, but nothing worked. Diana and I weren't talking much anymore; she had to care for her baby. Johnny and I had drifted apart a little bit. In any case, I didn't want to talk to or be around anyone at that time. It felt better to be alone. With no one to talk to and an empty heart, I found a new best friend—aspirins and any other pills I could find at the dollar store. They were the only things that I found pleasure in; they always seemed to make me feel better. There was no way I could live with that kind of feeling. I remember calling Johnny one day to talk; I felt so low, lower than scum. I needed to speak to someone, so I called Johnny.

"I can't talk right now, I have company," he said.

With no one to talk to, I made a trip to the dollar store next to the payphone that I called him from since I didn't have a house phone. I bought a bottle of aspirin and took at least ten of them with orange juice. It was the cheapest thing I could afford. I still didn't die, but I had a horrible stomachache and vomited. I didn't feel sad anymore, just pure physical pain. I didn't feel like I was empty anymore since those pills filled that empty spot inside my heart; they were my only way out. I had no life, none at all. I was better off dead. I saw people with moms, dads, siblings, families with a home, and they all seemed to take it for granted. Those people reminded me of myself. When I had a house in Haiti, I thought it was the way life was supposed to be. I never thought of life without those things. I took them for granted.

It was almost like someone was burning me alive, and the fire never went out—it just kept burning. The difference was it wasn't burning my skin. This fire was burning my soul, and that hurt more than the skin itself.

I lost all hope in life. I lost faith in God, and life wasn't worth living anymore. I had no control over the tears that continuously ran down my face; they were unstoppable. Only time would heal my heart and soul. The thing was, I didn't feel like I had a heart anymore, or a soul—they were crushed and trashed. My soul was destroyed; life had managed to ruin my poor soul. I should have never been born, never existed; life would've been better without me. I must have cried almost every night before going to bed in that studio, feeling empty. I wished my mom was still alive to tell me that things were going to be okay. I wanted to go to college, but that was never going to happen. I didn't have the strength to keep going.

I finally broke down. I wasn't strong anymore.

CHAPTER 13

AN ABUSIVE RELATIONSHIP

I finally gave up on being loved by family or parents; I finally realized that it was never going to happen. I wanted to have my own family, one where I could feel like I was wanted. I wanted a husband who was educated, of course, and a Christian. He didn't have to be handsome, but he had to love me. One child would be fine; maybe we could adopt another one. My new family would fill that gap inside my heart. I would never think about my mom or dad ever again. I would be happy, not empty or wanting to be loved, because I would now have too much of it. I thought it was that easy, but first, before I could work on building that family, I had to focus on educating myself.

That's when I met James, the guy who would change my life in a big way. I was almost twenty-one years old when I met James. He attended the community college close to where I lived;

he was studying Hospitality Management. James and I met at the store. James was born and raised in Texas, but his family moved to Georgia when he was in high school. James was of mixed race. He was over six feet tall and weighed close to two hundred pounds. He was charming, but not someone I would want to spend the rest of my life with. He didn't have the qualities that I wanted in a husband, but I liked spending time with him. He had a foul mouth and used profanity in nearly every sentence. Most of his friends had been in jail for petty crimes. I always dreamed of having a husband who would attend church with me. Someone who would wear dockers and boat shoes. I wanted a husband who spoke proper English. Someone who was edu-cated. James seemed to care for some reason. The first time we went out was to a Mexican restaurant where I ordered a chicken quesadilla, and he ordered tacos and a drink. He sat there admir-ing me; he made me feel so special, like I was worth something.

"You don't think I can make you happy, Cynthia?" he asked.

"I'm not sure," I said.

I could see in his eyes that he was serious; at that moment, I could see stars in his eyes. We then went for a walk where we talked about the future.

"I think I love you," he said. He wanted to give me the one thing that I had been searching for: love. I convinced myself that I could love him; it didn't matter if I didn't like him. I could grow to love him in the future. James knew I was a virgin and that I had never kissed a guy. He thought it was special. I was still hoping to keep my virginity until marriage.

A few weeks after meeting James, I let him kiss me. It was weird at first, but then I actually liked it. A few more weeks into our relationship, James and I had sex. I was no longer a virgin.

I expected to feel different. I expected to see stars, but I didn't feel much. Instead, I felt cheap and dirty. I did not feel different anymore. Not much separated me from everyone else I knew. I felt like I had disobeyed God. What if I didn't marry James? I would not be a virgin on my wedding night. What had I done? I had waited twenty-one years and clearly, I could have waited a few more years. But I think I was too angry at nature and at God. I was done playing the good girl game. I wanted to be a rebel.

So, I let James get his way most of the time. I let him kiss me when he wanted to, I let him choose where we went for a date, which movie we watched, I even let him decide what I ate when we went out. I thought it was so cool that someone cared enough to tell me what was good and bad. It didn't occur to me that I was giving him too much power. I wanted to be loved at any cost, and if it meant giving away some of my freedom, then I was willing to do so.

He started to tell me that he didn't like the way I did my hair, especially when I cut it. Then, one afternoon, while we were sitting together in my studio, talking about our future, he said, "I don't like your friends. I think you should stop talking to some of them. They're brainwashing you." I didn't have many friends anyway, so I wasn't sure where the statement came from. Most of my friends lived in other states. I had a few acquaintances from the church, and I would say a couple of them were friends.

"You can't tell me who to talk to," I told him. Next thing I knew, something hit me across the face. It was his keys. I held my face, crying, asking him why he did that. That was just a few weeks after we started dating."

"It was an accident," he said.

He begged for my forgiveness, telling me that it would never happen again. He later bought me a ring and flowers to prove that he was sorry for what he had done. That was the first sign I should have left James, because it was the beginning of a dangerous journey that could have ended with my death.

I forgave him because I thought he loved me; he would never hurt me again, I convinced myself. He never stopped telling me how beautiful I was and how he was so lucky to have me. He made me feel so special; I was the best thing that ever happened to him. How could I leave him for hurting me? After all, it was an accident. He didn't do it on purpose, I told myself. Besides, he didn't leave any scars that I would have to explain to people outside my home. No one needed to know. It was our secret. A dangerous one indeed.

Valentine's Day came, and I was sure James was going to get me something special. I had never gotten anything before from a boyfriend.

"I want a box of chocolate," I told him. He promised I would get it, and I did, but not like the one he got his mother. Hers was bigger; there was even candy on top of the box. Mine was just a small box of chocolate. I got jealous because his mother got something more special than I did. I wasn't trying to be petty, but I couldn't help the rage I felt inside—all the ghosts of Valentine's Day past held me in a chokehold.

"I want your mother's gift," I told him. I explained that I deserved the best because I was his girlfriend, the person he said he loved.

But he didn't care.

In a sudden fury, I later attempted to open his mom's box, and he pushed me on my bed and held my hands down.

"You're hurting me," I said.

"Stop fighting," he screamed.

Next thing I knew, he had his hand around my neck, and he threatened to squeeze if I didn't stop fighting. I was hoping he was kidding, but he wasn't. He pressed down on my neck, and I started crying. Tears just kept running from the corners of my eyes, and he stopped.

"You see what you made me do?" he asked.

I felt guilty that I'd made him mad. I blamed myself for making him hurt me again; he wouldn't have done it if I hadn't tried to open his mom's gift. *I should just keep my hands to myself next time; that'll make him happy.*

I made myself believe the first time was an accident and the second time was my fault. I would just have to try a little harder not to let it happen again. After all, I could prevent it from ever happening again if I just behaved. But the truth was none of it was my fault. There was no way I would ever be able to make James stop because everything he did was his fault, not mine. It wasn't my job to help him control his anger; it was his job. There was nothing I could have done to make him stop hurting me other than leave him and notify the authorities.

I thought it was my job to make him happy—all I had to do was give him what he wanted, no matter what it was. Then he started to yell at me for every little thing; he was becoming like Micho. Nothing I did was good enough in his eyes. I began to think of new ways to make him not get mad at me or push me. There were times when I even thought of leaving him, but that was not an option. Who else would love me? This guy cared about me, I reasoned, and all I had to do was make him happy. What if I left him and no one else loved me ever again? What would I do? As mean as he was half the time, he filled that hole inside my heart, and that alone was enough for me. Where would I go? What if he stalked me and killed me? Who would protect me? There was no place to hide unless I left the state.

One Sunday, James's parents invited me to attend a church service with them. James lived with his parents, but sometimes he spent the night at my place. Although I wasn't a Catholic, I didn't see anything wrong with going to church with them. James asked his parents if it was okay for me to sleep over the night before since their house was closer to the church. I went to their home that night feeling uncomfortable—I always preferred to sleep in my own bed—but they did their very best to put me at ease. His mom said she liked me because I always smiled; I was going to be a good wife someday, a responsible and caring one. I didn't only care about him, but I cared about his entire family, she thought.

The next morning was crazy. I decided to wear a blue dress with no sleeves. James wanted me to wear something over it, but I didn't want to.

"I don't want the guys at church to look at you," he said.

I refused, and he decided to give me another lesson. He pushed me into the bathroom and grabbed me by the neck.

"I said to wear something over it," he said, his teeth grinding.

I wanted to scream, but I didn't want his parents to hear; it would've been too embarrassing. I didn't want anyone to know what he was doing to me, so I stared at him with tears in my eyes until he decided to let go of me. I sat at the table with his family, nervous and sad, but no one knew how scared I was of this man who presented a perfect front to the world. I pretended like everything was fine. I smiled when everyone else smiled. I laughed when they did. Whenever a joke came up about James when he was a little boy, I pretended like I was so interested in what he was like, but deep inside, I hated him and what he was doing to me.

James was turning me into someone that I didn't want to be. He was making me live the life that I never wanted to live. I had promised myself that I would never live my mother's life and let a man have so much power over me. I'd told my mom that I was never going to be like her.

"If a man ever hits me, I'll kill him," I used to tell her as a child. And there I was getting abused, and I didn't know how to break free. He made me feel so weak, made me feel like nothing by telling me that no one really wanted me. He knew my weakness was to be loved.

"You will never find a man who loves you the way I do," he would say to me.

I thought of leaving him several times, but what if he was right? What if I never found someone to love me? What if I spent years with a man thinking that he loved me and ended up the way my mom did? I was willing to be beaten and degraded instead of being alone. If only Micho loved me, I thought; I wouldn't need to be with this monster. If only I had my family around to tell me that I was special and that things were going to be okay. Then I wouldn't believe James when he said that no one wanted me. Because he did have a point, I thought—no one wanted me. I'd lost everything: my mother, my dad, and my siblings. James was the only thing I had left. At least that's what I thought.

Months passed, and we had to go to the beach one weekend. I did not want to go in the first place, but I accepted at first to make James happy. After a long night, however, I was tired, so I decided that I wasn't going anymore. All I had to do was tell him, and he would understand. He showed up at my house, all dressed up in his shorts, ready for the beach.

"I'm not going anymore," I told him. "I don't feel well."

"Yes, you are," he said as if he owned me.

So I explained to him that I wasn't going and decided to go to bed. I turned my face when I saw his fist coming close to my head. He missed, but he wasn't done. A simple decision to no longer spend a day at the beach had turned into a reason for abuse. What made me think I had any power to make this man stop other than leaving him?

"I'm sick of this shit," he said. "You're trying to destroy my life."

I didn't see how I was trying to destroy his life; I thought it was the other way around. He was the one trying to ruin my life and turn me into someone that I wasn't. So I told him that I was sorry and that I would go if it made him happy, but he didn't want to go anymore. He said he was sick of me. He wanted to give me a lesson that I would never forget.

I dialed 911 as he ran to the door to lock it. The phone rang, but no one picked up. He grabbed the phone from me and cut the cord. So I ran to the door, screaming, "Help me!" I thought the cops would soon come. Although no one picked up, they had to know that someone called and didn't get through.

He ran after me and pushed me on the floor, kicking me and screaming, "Get up!" I got up, and he kept telling me to get in there. I didn't know what he was up to, but I knew I was going to do whatever he said. He grabbed me from behind and started choking me. I pushed him away with rage, gasping for air, but he was too strong for me and got a hold of my arm. I stood at 5 feet 3 inches and weighed around 109 pounds. I kept on screaming for someone to help me. I wanted a neighbor to call the police, but no one did. It wasn't their business; it was me and this monster. So I tried to convince him that I loved him and that I was sorry for whatever I did. I promised to do what he said from that moment on, but he didn't care. By then, an hour must have passed; the police never came, and no neighbor knocked on the door. I was losing strength. I couldn't scream anymore. I started to lose my voice. I figured if he was going to kill me, so be it. There was no way I could stop him from doing whatever was already on his mind.

I stood on the bed with my back on the wall, shaking, begging for him to stop. I started to remind him of the good times we had had together. I thought maybe he was afraid of me leaving him. I let him believe that I would never leave, no matter what, and that he and I were made for each other. But his eyes were blank. I could see Satan in his eyes. Nothing I said was registering with him. He picked up a pillow and started walking toward me. He was going to end it right there.

"You will never be able to destroy my life," he screamed, "you user."

I imagined the pillow on my face; I imagined myself gasping for air and not getting any. I imagined my body there, stiff and cold. I imagined the cops coming to investigate the crime scene, and I saw myself in a casket. I knew James was not going to stop because he had transformed into something else. He was no longer human. This day had been in the making for many months. I saw all the signs, and yet I stayed. I should have left when I had the chance. It was too late now. What was I going to do? That day, I was sure I was going to die a very painful death. The police would show up at some point; they were always late. James would get arrested and get charged with murder. He would probably have some regrets about what happened and feel sorry. But I would still be dead.

"My stomach hurts," I told him.

"I don't care," he said.

"Are you going to hurt your child?" I asked.

"You're not pregnant," he replied.

I finally got his weakness—it was a baby. He always wanted a child, and I knew that would do it. So I told him that I was pregnant, but he wanted to know why I never told him. I let him believe that I was waiting for the right time, a special time.

"Please don't kill the baby," I begged. I figured he didn't care about me, so I let him believe that I was protecting a part of him. He fell for it as he dropped the pillow on the floor and started crying.

I felt safe at that time; the pillow was on the floor, and he had tears in his eyes. It was my passport out of his life forever. I finally stepped off the bed and ran to the bathroom. First, I wanted to see my face; I wanted to see the damage he had done. It was swollen, sweaty, and bloody; my lips were busted. I had so many scars on my face. I started breathing hard, but my in-haler was nowhere to be found. I was diagnosed with asthma immediately after undergoing heart surgery, but I rarely needed to use my inhaler. Over the years, I had learned to abstain from things that could trigger an attack, like running or using cleaning products. I started shaking more and got weaker as I stared at my wounded face in the mirror. I walked over to the toilet bowl to spit, and I felt like I was going to puke.

Blood came out of my mouth, which scared me more. He came into the bathroom, still crying, begging for my forgiveness, as usual. He wasn't going to get it this time. I was done with him, but I would never tell him those words. It was my little secret; I just had to find a safe way to get out of the relationship. He started to tell me how sorry he was, how he would never do it again, like always. He then offered to carry me to the bed, and I accepted. He laid me down and never stopped staring at me.

"You see what you've done?" he asked. "Why do you make me do these things?"

By then, I knew better; I knew I wasn't responsible for his sick behavior. It was his weakness, not mine.

He sat next to me, telling me how he would let me go if I promised not to kill his child. I nodded to everything he said. Whatever he wanted me to do, I made him believe that I would do it. He already had a plan; he would leave me alone for a while. He would get some therapy so he wouldn't hit me anymore, but I would never be able to date another guy. If he couldn't have me, then no one else could.

I finally told Maria what was going on. I finally had the courage to let people know what was happening to me. I told Diana, and then Johnny. I wasn't ashamed anymore; it was about time people knew who he was. Diana offered to get me out of Georgia, and I accepted. Johnny was angry and asked if I wanted him to hurt James. I declined. I was more interested in leaving. No one else needed to get hurt, especially Johnny.

The next day, James showed up at my house again, but I wasn't there. I'd booked a flight to Massachusetts and was running some last-minute errands with Maria. I was going to leave him for good. Maria had offered to drive me to the airport. She dropped me off at the house to pick up some stuff while she went over to her house for a few minutes. She said she would return shortly.

A few minutes later, Maria showed up at my house. She was beside herself. She was alone.

"Where's the baby?" I asked.

"James is at my house, and he wants to exchange the baby for you."

Maria's son was nine months old at the time. By then Maria was no longer living with her sister. I wasn't about to go anywhere near him, so I decided to call the cops again. Although I got through that day, it didn't make much of a difference. The police couldn't come to my place because they were too busy. According to the operator, there were only two cops available, and they were both busy—I'd have to wait. I had to give them time, something that I didn't have.

I knocked on my neighbor's door, and thankfully, he answered. I told him I was afraid for my life and I needed his help.

"Didn't you hear me scream the other day?" I asked.

"Yes, but I didn't think anything was wrong," he replied.

"But I screamed for probably an hour," I told him. "I almost died."

At that point, he became concerned for my safety. I hid in his place and would remain there until the police showed up.

I called 911 again and explained to the operator what was going on. "You don't understand," I said, "this guy is dangerous." Still, there was nothing she could do to help me; I'd have to wait. My neighbor also called and explained the urgency to the operator, but we would have to wait. That day, I waited forty-five minutes before the police showed up, which was after I threatened to sue the town if anything happened to the baby or me.

One cop was African-American, and the other was Caucasian. The African-American officer asked, "Why are you with him?" That was not a question I could answer. All I knew was I needed to get as far away from him as possible and I needed the police to help.

The cops drove me to Maria's house, where James was still inside with her baby boy. The police cars pulled up, and James was ordered to come outside and give the baby to his mother. The officer spoke as if it was my fault that he tried to kill me! He never even took the time to ask James what his problem was and why he was hitting his girlfriend. I didn't understand the officer's question. I trusted them to protect me, but he was more interested in protecting the abuser. I guess, in a way, I allowed the abuse to continue because I could have left him earlier. I could have walked away before it got to that point. But I didn't have those answers at the time. I was trapped in that relationship and I hadn't known how to get out. But I did know how to get out that day.

The other officer was slightly different; he was more interested in filing a report and listening to what I had to say. He seemed to care about what had happened to me.

"What happened to her face?" the white officer asked James.

"I don't know," he said.

"What's wrong with you?" he asked James. "Why are you hitting a female?"

"It was an accident," he replied.

All I wanted was for him to leave me alone and move on with his life. I didn't even want him to go to jail. I didn't have the heart to put him there, but I wanted him to leave me alone, and he wouldn't do that. So, the officer asked James to put his hands behind his back and handcuffed him for lying—not for hitting me, but for lying about hitting me.

The officer tried to convince me to press charges. I could get a restraining order, a piece of paper that would keep him from coming near me. Just a piece of paper, I said to myself. I could call them if he ever came near me and show the paper to the cops—the same cops who didn't show up the day I nearly died, the same ones who came forty-five minutes late the day he held my friend's baby hostage. Did those people think I was crazy? I couldn't trust them; they'd failed to protect me when I needed them the most. I wasn't going to jeopardize my life again by listening to them. The police didn't arrest James that day because I didn't press charges. I wish they could have arrested and punished him without my help. I figured it would've been easier to get James out of my life if I didn't drag him to court, so I didn't press charges. Besides, I needed to leave the state and I would have to be in Atlanta to testify against him.

I missed my flight to Massachusetts that day. I had to buy another airline ticket for another day. I had nowhere to go that night. The cops left. I was not safe at Maria's house. James was free to return to my place after everything that happened. He agreed for me to move to Massachusetts while he got help for his anger.

I called Sheila and told her I had an emergency. I needed $200 immediately. Although we didn't really have any contact, she gave me the money. I was grateful to her for helping me when she didn't even know what I was going through. I went to a travel agency and bought a one-way ticket to Boston for the next day. My relationship with James lasted eight months. James and I agreed I would move back to Atlanta before the baby's birth. He still believed that I was pregnant, and I continued to lie.

CHAPTER 14

BACK TO MASSACHUSETTS

I decided to give Paul more details on what had happened. Maybe he would protect me from this monster who was trying to end my life. By then, Paul had his own place. He had rented a room from a Haitian lady. Paul's room was probably not much bigger than one hundred square feet with a twin-sized bed, a television, and a small table to hold his house phone. I did not stay with him.

Paul was furious when I told him about James. He wanted so much to hurt this guy for what he'd done to me. At first, I stayed with Diana. At the time, Diana was staying in a two-bedroom apartment with her mother and her young daughter. Diana's mom stayed in one room with Diana's daughter, and Diana and I stayed in the other room. I applied for work and got a job to work as a cashier at a retail store. The store mostly sold household items and clothing.

For weeks I let James believe that I was having his kid so he wouldn't hurt me again. James would call and ask how I was doing; he even started to see a therapist for his anger. He promised me he would change if I agreed to give him one more chance. There were times when I did think of giving him another chance, but I'm not sure what I was thinking.

About a month after I moved back to Salem, I left Diana's house and moved in with Paul. We shared a room together. The arrangement was not ideal, but it was what was necessary at the time. I had just gotten a job at a local gym where I worked at the front desk.

I worked between the hours of six a.m. and two p.m. I used to wake up early so I could catch the 5:30 bus two blocks from my house so I could get to work on time. Once I got to the gym, I would open the door and turn off the alarm system. The gym had a large fitness area with bikes, treadmills, weights, and other exercise equipment. There was a large pool behind the front desk area that was separated by a large glass wall. The gym had a women's locker room and a men's locker room. Apart from opening the gym on weekdays, my job consisted of swiping members' cards and receiving payments from those who opted to pay in person. Although the front desk didn't have a chair and I had to stand my entire shift, I enjoyed that job. I got to meet people from various backgrounds and ethnicities. Most of the people who attended the gym in the morning were professionals who came to exercise before heading to the office. They always took the time to thank me for coming in so early to open for them. That job made me feel like I had a purpose.

James called my house one afternoon and got Paul instead. By then, he knew that Paul was aware of everything that had happened, so he took the opportunity to apologize for his behavior. He told Paul that he would never hurt me again.

"If you ever come close to my sister again, I'll kill you," Paul said.

It felt so good to know that someone was willing to protect me. That was one weight lifted from my shoulders.

James refused to leave me alone. He thought I had something that belonged to him, so he wasn't about to leave me alone until he got what he wanted.

"There's no baby, you dummy," I told him.

"What?" he said.

"I lied."

"I should've killed you when I had the chance."

I don't think I realized how bad the relationship was until I heard the echo of those words in my ears. I kept hearing them repeatedly; he should have killed me when he had the chance—a chance that I'd been willing to give him again and again.

For months, I'd thought his behavior had been my fault. I thought it was my responsibility to fix things. I'd made it my job to make the relationship work. I thought I was the weak one. But I was wrong. James was the weak one, and he'd used his weakness to degrade me and make me feel like I was scum. All those times I felt like I needed him, I felt like no one else was ever going to want me beside him, I was so wrong. I started to read books on domestic violence. The more I read, the more I realized that none of it had been my fault. James was the bad guy, and I was his victim—a survivor, I should say.

I learned so much from dating him: I learned to never judge another person for not being able to walk away from an abusive relationship. I learned that love doesn't have to hurt. I learned that I didn't make him do those things to me. I learned that I was stronger than I thought I was since I was able to walk away and let others know what had happened. I learned that I wasn't made for one man, and I didn't have to stick it out because someone claimed he was the best man for me. I learned to look for signs of anger and control—the only way I'd avoid another situation in the future—and maybe help someone else in a similar situation. My relationship with James had two possible endings: I could either leave it, or he would have killed me. I wish I had known that before the traumatic experience of him nearly ending my life.

I moved back to Massachusetts just five months after Sheila and I split. It was also just a few months after my mother died. Just two days after I was almost killed. By the time I made it to Salem, Sheila and I had started talking again, but there wasn't any real connection; it just didn't feel right to me. I'd left everything in Georgia, which was almost nothing. I'd moved with nothing but a few clothes and shoes. I wanted to start fresh and leave all my baggage behind, including my past life.

Although I knew why I'd left Georgia, I didn't want to stay in Massachusetts. The problem was never in another state; it was inside my heart. I realized that no matter where I moved, my pain was going to follow me. I started to hang out with a guy who called himself Pretty Boy. Pretty Boy was our neighbor and worked as a delivery driver. Pretty Boy was hot. He promised to drive me around. I saw him almost every day, and he called me every night. "I think you're a special woman; be my girlfriend," he would say. At first, I was hesitant, but he was so handsome and smooth.

Although I promised myself not to date anyone anytime soon, I couldn't help it. This guy was too charming. He was biracial—African-American and Puerto Rican. He was light-skinned, with short curly hair, big brown eyes, beautiful clean teeth, and he was muscular. I had such a weakness for beautiful teeth. At thirty years old, Pretty Boy lived with his father and was only interested in working to make money. He didn't go to school, and he didn't like to read. He preferred to be with different women, but I didn't know it at the time.

It was maybe a week after my birthday that I visited Pretty Boy for the first time at his place. Pretty Boy was on his bed, and I was on the floor talking about nothing. I am not even sure why I went there, but there wasn't much to do when I was not at work. Paul and I didn't have enough money to get cable, so we could not watch television unless we popped a video home system (VHS) tape inside the video cassette recorder. That was before digital video disks (DVDs) and the internet were popular.

Pretty Boy leaned over at the edge of his bed to look at me. I was lying on my back on the floor. "You are so beautiful," he said.

I was shy, so I smirked. *Gosh this guy was handsome,* I thought to myself.

"I'm serious; I would do anything to have you as my girl-friend," he said.

He was handsome. I liked him a lot, plus it wasn't like he was a stranger. He and Paul had become good friends. I told myself that he would never hurt me. Why would he hurt his friend's sister?

I was getting ready to leave when Pretty Boy got up to walk me to the door. "Give me a kiss," he said. He got so close to me that my legs and arms were shaking. I was speechless. I wanted to kiss him, but I didn't know how to start. He touched my stomach and repeated it, "C'mon, baby, kiss me," and he kissed my neck.

There was something about his smell; I'm not sure what type of cologne he wore, but whatever it was, it was different, and it gave me goose bumps. I got so excited, but I didn't want to do anything with him, so I asked to leave, but he kept on touching me. I think I was in love because I never said stop. I almost cried after kissing him because I was afraid he was going to break my heart. I knew I was going crazy for him, and once I gave him the key to my heart, he could come and go as he pleased and do lots of damage. I allowed Pretty Boy to kiss me that day. He was a good kisser too. But that's as far as it went.

Now I felt like the happiest woman on the planet; I had a place to live, a job I liked, and a boyfriend I adored. I didn't feel depressed anymore, and I was no longer empty inside, because someone or something had filled that gap inside my heart. I didn't know what it was, but I liked it. Besides, I had my god-daughter, Sonya, around to make me laugh whenever I got a little sad. Now there was one thing left to be done—go to school at a university where I could prepare for a better future. All the friends I had from middle school were going to school except for me, but I would soon change that.

It was harder than I thought.

One day, I caught the public bus to the local community college so I could apply for school and for financial aid. I had already gone to the registrar's office, where I provided proof of residency so I could pay in-state tuition. I had already chosen a field of study, which would be English. The only thing left was to decide how I was going to pay for school.

I walked over to the financial aid office, which was located just a few feet away from the registrar's office. A counselor asked me to sit down so she could look at my documents. She gave me a list of things that I would need in order to qualify.

"How old are you?"

"Twenty-one," I replied.

I was nearly twenty-two by then. Old enough to be a senior in college. She asked for my parents' income tax return. "I don't have any parents," I replied. "My mother's dead, and my father is not in my life." She asked who I lived with. "My brother," I replied.

"You're not independent," the counselor said to me. "You won't be qualified for financial aid unless your parents sign this form."

What was that? Maybe I didn't hear her correctly. I couldn't get help to pay for my education because I didn't have parents? Wouldn't that be more of a reason to give me help? At first, I thought she was kidding, but I soon realized that she wasn't joking when she gave all my documents back to me. I walked out of that office with tears in my eyes. It was almost time for school to start, and if I wanted to start that semester, I had to get things done right away. I had to act quickly. Although I was independent because I took care of myself, I was considered a dependent because I was not yet twenty-four years old. Who the hell created that rule? I was not an orphan or a ward of the court, so the answer was no.

So, I did something that I never thought I would do: I asked Micho for help. Not for money, but his signature on a financial aid form since he was my father. Since Micho was living below the poverty line, I would still be qualified for financial aid.

"Sure," he said, "just bring the form over, and I'll sign it." I thanked him for agreeing to help and said I would call before going there on Saturday.

When Saturday came, I called to tell him I was on my way.

"No," he said. "I can't do that anymore. I got some useful information from people who know how those things work, and they told me that I don't have to sign it because you're already eighteen."

Now, I was thinking, *this guy is kidding.* "Papa," I said. "I have already gone to the school office and I can't sign on my own because I am under twenty-four years old." That day, Micho stood his ground and said no, he would not help me.

"No, they'll give it to you," he said, so I told him to forget it.

Now I was back to square one. Although I had a place to live, a job, and a handsome boyfriend, I didn't have the most important thing that I wanted: an education. I returned to see the financial aid counselor again, to beg her for mercy. Maybe she didn't understand me the last time. I offered to bring her affidavits certifying that my mother was dead and my father was not in my life. In the end, her hands were tied; there was nothing she could do to help. The system didn't appear to have anything in place for people in my position. Nothing could be done, and nothing was done. If only I had known about emancipation, I would have asked a judge to declare me independent. But no one told me this was an option.

Paul was very supportive when I stayed with him; he managed to save enough money to buy a car, and he gave me a ride whenever he could. But I started to have that funny feeling in my stomach again. By then, I had left the job at the fitness center and had started working at a clothing store at the mall. That cloud returned over my head, and my life was dark all over again. I needed to see the light, but I didn't know how to get to it. I started to cry almost every night before going to bed. I never told my brother, but he saw me crying in the bathroom one night. I couldn't hide it, I just couldn't take it anymore, it was too much for me to bear. I hated my life again; it just wasn't worth living anymore. I wanted to die, but death didn't want me.

"Don't cry, you're going to make me cry too," Paul said.

There was no way I could stop. It was almost like someone kept stabbing me in the heart and didn't want to stop. The only way I could stop crying was to not be alive anymore and disappear from this planet like I'd never been here. That would have been much better than trying to make life better. Besides, life didn't want me to be a part of it. I guess it didn't know how to get rid of me either. Otherwise, it would have done it a long time ago. I had to find a new way to go to school. There had to be another way because the usual way just wasn't working.

I never did find a job in a doctor's office so my medical secretary certificate was useless to me at that point. As my life spiraled out of control, Nadia and her family watched from the sidelines. One day while I was walking, Esther drove by and stopped to say hello. I didn't have money to buy a car, so I still caught the bus.

"Why didn't you stay in Georgia like your sister did?" she asked. Why was I even talking to Esther? She was now my dad's step-daughter, but it didn't make her anything to me. She was nothing to me, just like her mother was nothing to me. I don't even know why I stopped to talk to her that day. Although Esther and I were the same age, she had started college and was getting ready to finish her last year.

I was doing exactly what Nadia and her family expected me to do. I wasn't going to school, and I was dating a guy just because he was cute. They were right all this time; I was everything they said I was—a slut, a hypocrite, and a loser. I had absolutely no life. I had even lost touch with God, and the church was the last place I wanted to visit. To make matters worse, Pretty Boy started acting like his real self, not keeping his word, coming two hours late when we had a date, and not caring. The fact that he had changed should not have been a big deal, I should have been able to drop him and move on, but I couldn't. I depended on him too much for emotional support; I needed him to fill that gap inside my heart because I didn't know how to find the strength within myself.

My life was falling apart, and in my mind, things were never going to get any better. I was cursed, and I was sick of being me. I knew other people who had normal lives. Why wasn't I one of those people? All I wanted was to be somebody in life with a career—to have a good life. I wanted to be able to buy a house, have a job that I loved and that paid well. I wanted to have health insurance and be able to run my own business.

I went back to God and started attending a nondenominational church in Salem. Pretty Boy attended the same church with his family. One Sunday afternoon, Pretty Boy was supposed to pick me up for church; he didn't show up and didn't call. It wasn't the first time he had lied to me, so by then, I got the idea that he just didn't care anymore. I wasn't wanted anymore, and all of a sudden everything came back—all of it.

I was sitting in the room, crying, as usual, the hammer was smashing my heart again. I felt like there was a rope tied around my neck, and I couldn't breathe. It was almost like someone had forced me into a small, dark room with no air. I needed to break free, but I didn't know how to get out. I was too helpless by then, I was too weak, and I didn't have any energy left inside of me.

I hated my life. I hated the fact that I didn't have family members who cared. I missed having a mom. I wished I had a dad. I knew I had a father alive, but he wasn't a dad. I wished I had people who loved me, and since my family didn't, I wanted Pretty Boy to love me. Although I lived with Paul at the time, he had his own life. He couldn't tell what was happening in mine. He wouldn't understand if I told him because mental illness was not considered a real illness in my community. People thought of it as something someone could just stop thinking about. It was all in the mind. A delusion, not reality. Occasionally, Paul saw me crying and he would wrap his arm around me and say things would be okay, but he did not know how deep the pain hurt.

I felt like I was going to die, that something was killing me slowly, and I wanted it to end quickly. It was too slow and painful all at once. I sat in the room, and all I could see was darkness. There was no light; everything was ugly and bad, just like me. When I looked around the room, I saw myself and nothing else. I didn't want any friends around me, nor people who faked loving me. So, I turned to the one thing that had always been able to make me feel better—pills, which were mostly aspirins because they only cost one dollar for a bottle. I must have taken fifteen pills that day with orange juice, and as soon as I took them, the emotional pain went away. It was so amazing. I had found a way of making the feeling subside.

Now, although I didn't have the psychological pain anymore, I had physical pain. My stomach started hurting, and I honestly thought I was going to die. The pain was excruciating. It was almost like someone was cutting my stomach into pieces with a knife. I picked up the phone and dialed 911. The room was spinning with me. I couldn't even talk to tell the operator what was wrong. All of a sudden, everything was quiet, and I dropped the phone on the floor. Unlike my experience with the police in Atlanta, the police did show up at my house in Salem that night. My eyes were still open, although I was too weak to speak. I'm not sure how the police officer got into the house, but he did walk into my room.

"Are you okay?" the police officer asked.

I did not say anything back, but he called for an ambulance. That night, the paramedics came into the room and placed me on a stretcher. They wheeled me out of the house and into the ambulance. By then, several neighbors had gathered outside to see what was going on. The paramedics took me to the local hospital where I was seen in the emergency room for stomach pain and nausea. Once I got to the emergency room, the pain intensified. At one point, I felt like I was going to pass out, and at the same time, it felt like my stomach was about to explode from being inflated. The nurses gave me a kidney dish in case

I needed to vomit. A few minutes later, I felt like I needed to defecate. I rushed to the bathroom and sat on the toilet, my legs shaking from pain. I leaned forward with my hand squeezing my stomach to minimize the pain. I wanted someone to take the pain away.

"Help," I kept shouting. A few minutes later, I vomited all over the bathroom floor. The more I vomited, the better I felt. I could taste the orange juice and the aspirins as my body purged them out through my mouth and nose.

The doctor thought I might have been pregnant, but the pregnancy test came back negative. I couldn't have been pregnant anyway because I was not sexually active.

"You have an infection in your blood," the doctor said, but she didn't know what it was. She wanted to know what I had eaten that day—maybe I was allergic to something or had food poisoning. She wanted to perform a test similar to a pap smear to check what was going on inside of me, but I declined.

Micho showed up in the hospital room that night. I'm not sure how he found out that I was even there. He wanted to know what was wrong with me, but I'd already told the doctor not to tell anyone what was wrong with me except for Paul. No matter how much Micho tried, the doctor denied a response. My dad seemed like he cared that day, but I already knew what was on his mind: he wanted to come to see me and report back to Nadia and her family.

I stayed in the hospital for maybe four hours that night. My stomach was still hurting, although I was given an IV. It was around midnight when Paul came to visit; the doctor told him I was ready to go home. My stomach was still hurting, I could barely stand, and I was sweating profusely. I could not walk, but she said I had to go home. Maybe it had to do with the fact that I didn't have health insurance. I was a non-paying patient, as usual.

That night when Paul and I got our room, he placed a mattress on the floor to sleep on; I could not even get to the bed. Pretty Boy came to visit; he wanted to know what had happened. He stayed the night, sleeping most of it while I was awake, and left the next morning around five.

"How's the baby?" Jephte asked the next day.

He had called to see how I was doing. By then, I didn't have much contact with Nadia's kids, although I would not say we were enemies.

"What baby?" I answered with surprise, not knowing what was going on.

Although I didn't care for Nadia, I had always liked Jephte. He was always nice to me, so I let it slide. No one told me what was going on, but apparently, word was going around that I was pregnant—that's why I'd been vomiting in the hospital that night.

I liked living in Massachusetts, and I wasn't going to let anyone stop me, ever. No matter how hard they tried, it was never going to work—I wasn't going to let them get the best of me. I was in control of my life now, or at least I thought I was. Whatever happened in my life from that moment on was up to me and no one else.

I spent most of that week eating saltine crackers and drinking ginger ale. My stomach felt horrible. I wished Micho had the guts to ask instead of making things up. If only he had asked me, I would have told him there was never any baby, not that he would have believed me because he already had his mind made up. The only thing that kept going through my mind was that Micho and his new family were out to destroy me. If I wasn't going to destroy myself, they would make it seem like I was.

I became paranoid. They wanted the world to see that I was the slut that they always thought I was. I didn't go to school and had a job where I made six dollars an hour. I wasn't married, and I was supposedly pregnant, so that made me the loser they always said I was. Years later, some of them would still think that I'd been pregnant and had had an abortion.

I couldn't stop wondering why people had to be so cruel, hurting others to satisfy themselves. I just didn't get it; maybe I was never going to get it. It just didn't make sense to me. Their number one dream was for me to have a baby without a father and go on welfare, but that wasn't my dream. Someone once told me, "Words can only hurt you if you let them," but it's funny how much words can hurt. They not only hurt, but they can also destroy someone's soul. They did mine. The words that were said about me hardened my heart like a stone, to the point where I was unable to love or feel. They numbed me to the point where I was living as if I were dead when I still had life inside of me.

I guess I got to the point where I wanted to be loved, even if it was by someone who couldn't love me; I would have done anything to feel loved. Even if it were only for a few minutes, I would have been satisfied. I guess that's why I thought I loved Pretty Boy, and I thought he loved me too, even though he treated me like his doormat. I wanted to be with him just to have someone close to my heart. I liked the idea of being loved, although it wasn't love.

I started to settle for less than what I deserved. I stopped talking about what I wanted since I didn't even know what I wanted anymore. I wanted nothing out of life; I didn't even want life itself. I can't even remember how many times Pretty Boy hurt me, and I tolerated him. I knew he was cheating—a few neighbors told me—but I said to myself that I was his favorite because he spent most of his time with me.

One day Pretty Boy came over and told me he had something serious to tell me.

"A girl I was dating is pregnant," he said. I was shocked. What was I supposed to do with this information? But Pretty Boy assured me that he would take care of the baby and wanted nothing to do with the girl. That was the moment I was supposed to leave him. What kind of man was willing to get a woman pregnant and walk away to be with someone else? And what made me think he would treat me any differently? Unfortunately for me, I didn't leave Pretty Boy. I accepted the fact that this young girl would go through a pregnancy alone while her baby's father would spend the majority of his time with me. How much crueler could I have been? They had already broken up, I thought to myself. He was mine now.

No matter what Pretty Boy did, I always took him back into my life because I liked the idea of the person I wanted him to be, but not the person that he was. By the time I realized he was not the right guy, he had already crushed my heart. I couldn't feel anything anymore, and I hated men. Pretty Boy never hit me physically. He never told me I wasn't good enough. I don't think he ever yelled at me. But in a sense, my relationship with him was abusive because he abused my feelings. The girl never got pregnant with Pretty Boy's baby; it was just a tactic he used to make me think he was no longer in a relationship with her when he was. By the time I found out Pretty Boy had lied, he had already hurt me and the girl. He played us both for fools.

At twenty-two years old, I felt like I had had it with men. I didn't want to have any more of them, especially a Haitian one. After all, Micho was Haitian, and he screwed my mother up. *I must have bad luck with men*, I used to say to myself. What was wrong with me? Why didn't anyone love me? What could I do to make someone love me? Everyone who had ever told me they loved me had broken my heart or died. I didn't even know what love was supposed to feel like anymore.

Sometimes I thought I felt love with Johnny, but I wasn't sure that's what it was. I knew it was supposed to feel good, that I was only supposed to feel it, not see it. But Micho had fed me since the day I was born, he paid my school, got me a green card, he must have loved me. Maybe I was the problem. Perhaps I did something wrong to make people dislike me. But then again, why was Johnny so fond of me? If I was so bad, why did he love me so much? I knew there had to be something good about me for someone to love me the way Johnny did.

I remember one afternoon, it was Paul's birthday, and I cooked him a special meal: traditional Haitian rice with black mushrooms, chicken, potato salad with beets (we call it "salade russe" or Russian salad in Haiti), and baked macaroni. Diana called earlier that day; she wanted to hang out after work. When she came over that afternoon, she changed her mind after speaking to her boyfriend. I was furious. I felt like she only wanted to hang out with me when she had no plans, but once her boyfriend asked her to go out, she bailed out on me. So we got into a small argument with about five of Paul's friends present.

"You can't do that," I told her. "You promised to hang out with me."

"Well, you're not my man, so I can't be hanging out with you all the time," she said.

Ouch! Everyone laughed; they thought it was funny. I didn't find it funny, so I asked her to leave.

"If I leave, I'll never come back," she said.

"Fine," I told her.

I slammed the door behind her, and everyone stopped laughing. Paul asked me to go after her, but I didn't. She was my best friend, I loved her like a sister, and she should never have said those words to me. Paul finally went outside to talk to her; she was still sitting in her car. I'm not sure what they talked about during that time because I never asked. My self-esteem was so low that things that I could have brushed off became triggers to my depression.

I remember being at the Community College one afternoon. Diana parked her car across the street from where I was. I had been waiting for the bus. I went there to use the computer lab as a guest. Sonya was with her, and I wanted so much to go over and say hi, and hold Sonya in my arms, but I didn't. I had too much pride. I was afraid she would not have allowed me to play with the child.

A couple of months later, I got a call early in the morning. It was Diana, and she was crying.

"I just had a dream," she said. "I miss you so much."

"I miss you too," I said. I apologized.

From that day on, we went back to being friends like nothing had happened. I didn't want to dwell on the past.

One afternoon, Pretty Boy and I were supposed to attend church, and he didn't show up. This made me nervous and scared because I liked him a lot. I was still hoping we could work. That afternoon, I sat in the room I shared with Paul and cried uncontrollably. I felt hopeless and just tired of everything life had thrown at me. Pretty Boy came over and informed me he was moving out of state. What? Where did that come from? So that day, I offered to make him some spaghetti. He refused and said he didn't have time. He had to go.

"When was this decided?" I asked. He didn't have a good answer other than he was leaving town. I begged him to reconsider. I loved him. But he showed no emotions.

"I am sorry," he said. "I never meant to hurt you."

But you see, he did mean to hurt me. I felt crushed. I watched Pretty Boy leave with little emotion on his end, like he never cared at all. That night I made the decision to work on myself, no more boyfriends for a while. I needed to find out who I was and why I was always so empty inside.

CHAPTER 15

RECLAIMING MY LIFE

Now that both James and Pretty Boy were completely out of my life, I decided to focus on what was more important to me—getting an education and pulling myself out of poverty. As soon as I settled in Salem, I completely cut contact with James. He didn't know where I was staying, and as far as I was concerned, he couldn't hurt me anymore. By then, I had already lived in Massachusetts for at least one year. I worked several jobs, including as a cashier at a supermarket, and a few retail stores at the mall, trying to make ends meet.

I reapplied to the local community college. I had to face the same financial aid woman who had denied me the year before. What would I tell her this time? Micho and I were not talking. I had been ignoring him since he declined to help me with my FAFSA application. It would be another two years before I could get financial aid on my own without anyone's help. By then,

Nadia and Micho were already husband and wife and living together. I swallowed my pride and asked Nadia for help.

"Of course," she said. Nadia gave me a time and day to meet at her house and I went. I was desperate. I was willing to do anything to start school. I would have done anything except prostitution. Nadia agreed to sign my FAFSA application and gave me a copy of her income tax return. No one was ever supposed to find out what she had done for me. Not even Micho. No one was ever supposed to find out her income, not even Micho. I promised to return her documents as soon as the financial aid officer finished with them. The same lady who had denied me a year earlier looked me in the eye and told me I was approved. Financial aid would cover my tuition, and I would receive a refund that I could use to pay for books and transportation to and from school.

Nadia was happy to hear that I was approved. I was grateful to Nadia. I hated the fact that I had to go to her for help. She had hurt me so many times in the past. But at that point, I wanted to get an education more than I disliked her. I had made a deal with the devil. How could I have? What was I thinking? Why did she help me? Was it shame? Maybe God was looking out for me after all.

When I finally went to school, it was harder than I thought. At first my major was English, but what would I do with such a degree? I was a poor Haitian girl who had only spent five years in middle school and high school learning English. Could I be a journalist? A writer? A teacher? I didn't think I could be a teacher. I was an introvert. I did better when I was alone. Quiet time was too important to me. So, I switched to business. I needed something that could provide me with a job soon after graduation so I could get out of poverty. For some reason, I had too much going on in my head to understand what the professors were saying. I knew what I wanted—I had been waiting for it for a very long time—but the moment I had it, I didn't know how to handle it. I don't know what made me believe that going to school was all I needed to be happy because it added to my stress instead of relieving it. I took a biology class, which I later dropped because I missed the first class and could not keep up with the work. English was my favorite subject; I enjoyed writing essays, especially those I got to write about myself. I ended up dropping out the first semester before midterms; I just could not handle it. There was still this big gap inside my heart, and going to school wasn't the right remedy—at least not at the time. I didn't go the following semester either, so that was another year lost.

I remember sitting in the room I shared with Paul one night, and the same feelings started to come back—that cloud hung over my head like a fog, and that hammer was smashing my heart all over again. I couldn't stop the tears from running down my cheeks. I missed my mom so much that night. I needed her shoulder to cry on; I needed her to tell me that things were going to be okay. I didn't want to die anymore. I knew things could get better, but I didn't know how or when it was going to happen. I was losing patience; I was angry and hopeless. That night, although I knew I was never going to see my mom again, I wished I had a grave close by to visit. I believed she would not have been able to hear me, but it probably would've made me feel better. For me to go to where her body lay would have comforted me a lot, but I had nothing except for her pictures.

I went to bed thinking that tomorrow was going to get better. At least that's what I made myself believe so I could fall asleep. I woke up the next day feeling more horrible. I didn't want to see another day, another hour, another minute, another second. I had been feeling like that for a long time, and since I didn't know how to get rid of the feeling on my own, I finally realized that I needed some professional help. I had tried to apply for Medicaid more than once and was denied each time. The last time I applied, I was working part-time at a retail store at the mall. I wanted to see a cardiologist. At the time, I made less than $400 a month. The social worker said I made too much money. It made no sense to me at the time. I am not sure if she was lying or if she was really following the state's guidelines. Being poor made it harder to get help because there was no money to see a doctor who could have referred me to a therapist for emotional help.

By then, I knew what I wanted: an education to pull myself out of poverty, health insurance (I hadn't seen a doctor in years for my heart), and a new place to live. I wanted to be happy, so I called the suicide hotline for help.

"I need to speak to a doctor," I said, sobbing on the phone.

"What's the problem?" the woman on the line asked.

"I don't know," I replied. As usual, I didn't know why I had this feeling inside of me.

The operator offered to send a car to get me, but I refused. I told her I would get there myself. But I only half meant it.

A few minutes after I made the call, I noticed there were fire trucks outside the house. I stepped outside to see what was going on, and I saw smoke. My next-door neighbor's house was on fire, and two people were trapped inside. So I thought to myself, while I was thinking about how I couldn't live anymore, two other people wished they weren't in that furnace. I stood there, praying and waiting for them to be safe. I wanted the firefighters to get them out of there soon before they die. I waited until both of them were carried out of the burning house, covered with blankets, and led to an ambulance.

I decided right then to go to the closest mental health hospital in my town, a few minutes from my house. I had to get rid of these thoughts once and for all. On the bus to the hospital, I looked at everyone's faces—some of them were laughing, others were serious—and I wondered if they knew how sick I was of life.

"Everything will be okay soon," I told myself. I was going to take care of myself for once; I would make sure I never had such thoughts again.

Walking into the hospital was so easy, but I didn't know that leaving it was going to be so difficult. When I walked in, the office looked like a real emergency room, with a waiting area for patients expecting to see the doctor. The secretaries were right across from the front door, and they gave me a form to fill out, asking me some basic questions before I was sent to the waiting area.

"On a scale of one to ten, how much do you want to die?" the psychiatrist asked when I entered his office.

"A nine," I said.

"I can't let you leave this hospital," he said. "The law gives me the right to keep you here if you are a danger to yourself. Now, you have two options: you can sign yourself in and check yourself out in three days—or I will check you in and only let you out when I think you're able to take care of yourself."

I was thinking he couldn't be serious, so I asked him, "What if I wanted to walk out right now, what would you do?"

"I would stop you; we have guards all around. Besides, the doors are all locked," he said.

Once again, he outlined the only two choices I had: I could sign myself in and be released in three days. Otherwise, he would admit me to the hospital himself; the staff would then evaluate me, and I'd be released whenever the staff thought I was ready to be in the real world. I wanted to be tough, I didn't want him to win, but I figured he would win either way. I'd given him power over me the moment I'd stepped foot in his hospital.

I told him I wished I'd never come in. "I should've stayed home," I told him. I even thought it was illegal for a moment—he couldn't possibly keep me in a place without my consent—but then he explained that I wasn't safe around myself, so it was for my own good. He was right, it was not safe for me to be alone. I weighed my options and decided to play it smart, so I signed myself in. Once the papers were signed, I had to go inside the real hospital, where all the guards stood. I would not see outside again until they decided it was safe. It felt like a jail. I felt trapped.

The first guy I saw there was Haitian; he had such a thick accent. He was trying to be tough when he told me to sit down. He told me all the rules, things like, "If you don't eat or shower, or if you don't take your medicine, they will put you in a vest." I found that information to be irrelevant at the time; I was going to get out of that place one way or another.

There I met all kinds of people, and one of them I even knew. Everyone in there looked like they were on medication; they looked calm and drowsy, some too hyper and others too sleepy.

I knew I needed help, but I did not want to be on medication. I knew it was going to make me worse. All I needed was a better home and some money to get by; then, I would be okay.

That night I was placed in a room with an older lady who had multiple personalities. The room was small. There were two twin-sized beds. A short curtain separated her side from mine. The lady constantly talked to herself. It scared me a bit. I didn't want her imaginary friends to convince her to harm me. That was even scarier to me than thinking of taking my life. The lady in charge of watching the room that night was also Haitian. She was the one who told me the Caucasian lady had multiple personalities and could not be left alone. The Haitian lady had a thick accent. She sat at the entrance of the room to supervise. She ignored me until she found out about our shared homeland.

"What are you doing here?" she asked.

"I'm suicidal," I replied.

She thought I was too young to be suicidal, or even be depressed, so she said to me, "If you were my kid, I would whip you for even having those thoughts."

"If I were your kid, I wouldn't be so empty. I would probably be in my bed at home, not thinking about not seeing another day because life was so hopeless," I replied.

I could see tears in her eyes, and she changed the topic.

The next day, I went to a big room that looked like a recreation area. People lined up to get their medications. Each one received a small cup with their pills and another small cup of water. One by one, they were ordered to take the pill in front of the attendant and then open their mouth so the attendant could verify they had actually swallowed the pill. I felt terrified. Was I going to be forced to swallow a pill as well? They didn't call my name. I was relieved. As much as I needed help, I was not sure the answer to my problems was to take more pills.

That morning, I saw a psychologist and a psychiatrist. There were two other people in the room, but I didn't know who they were—maybe social workers observing what was going on? I had a key chain hanging around my neck with the abbreviation WWJD.

"Do you know what your key chain says?" one of the women asked.

"Yes," I replied. "What Would Jesus Do?"

"Well, what do you think Jesus would do to you if you killed yourself?"

"He would send me to Hell."

Throughout the whole session, I had a smile on my face. The staff looked more miserable than I was.

"Why are you smiling?" one asked.

"I don't know."

"You keep hiding your fears with your smile. It's not a good thing."

"I don't know. I'm not hiding anything with my smile," I said. If I wanted to get out of that place, I needed to act normal. I wanted to pretend like everything was okay. Make them believe that I was not a threat to myself or anyone else. I knew I needed help. I wanted help. But I didn't want to be stuck in a place that felt like jail. There was nothing loving about that place. The employees were like prison guards. The walls felt like prison bars. From what I saw earlier, they were only helping people by medicating them. I needed a home, food to eat, health insurance, a decent job, and money. I wanted to be happy for once in America. Would they give me Medicaid? How about food stamps?

Would they help me pay for a place so I did not have to share a room with Paul and sleep on a box spring? How about a car? I was tired of catching the bus during the brutal winter months. Some days I could barely feel my toes.

They wanted to know why I was so sad and angry, but I couldn't tell them because I didn't know the reason. It was just something that I could feel but was unable to explain. I just could not seem to put my finger on it. I was so embarrassed—I couldn't control my own life, so someone else had to take charge of it. Paul visited and brought me some clothes. He promised not to tell anyone. I guess it's always been an embarrassment in my culture to be in a mental institution.

There, I met a guy named Chad, an American guy who was utterly depressed because he didn't have his family around. He'd been homeless, hungry, and dirty; he had gone through it all. I was glad I met Chad because he helped me cope during those three days—we joked, watched television together, and told each other our troubles. Chad stood at around 5'8" and weighed around 170 pounds. He was missing one of his two front teeth. He looked like he was not much older than twenty-five years old. Chad seemed to understand me more than anyone else, including the shrinks, because he'd been through loss himself. I remember one afternoon we sat in the yard, talking about why we hated life so much.

"You have such a tight and sexy body," he said. The only thing I could do was laugh at his statement, but it also felt good to know that someone thought I looked beautiful even if he wasn't my type. I don't think it was the fact that he liked my body that mattered; I was just glad he was interested in me. He thought I was beautiful, and that mattered. It made me realize that if someone liked me, no matter who it was, there had to be something special about me. At least that's what I made myself believe at the time. It was a temporary feeling as my self-esteem went from high to low from time to time.

Three days later, they decided that I was sane, so I signed myself out. It was like buying time until the next crisis. Some outpatient therapy would do it for me, but since I didn't have medical insurance, they would try to get me Medicaid to cover the medical bill for those three days. What a blessing that would have been. With Medicaid, I could finally have a primary physician and see a cardiologist.

I went to the social services office to apply for Medicaid again. This time the mental health hospital referred me to a social worker at the Department of Social Services. I informed the social worker that I had applied for Medicaid before and been denied. She asked me some questions related to my health history and my financial situation. I explained to her that I was making under $400 a month working part-time at a retail store, and I shared a room with my brother.

Anne was her name. She was a middle-aged Caucasian lady, probably in her fifties. She was sweet and seemed concerned that her office had refused to help me in the past. She kept telling me she didn't understand why I had been denied Medicaid. She seemed to care. Anne walked my file over to another office and asked me to wait at her desk. I could hear her ask the lady to explain why I had been denied Medicaid in the past. Within thirty minutes, they determined that I was eligible. I was approved. Someone would have to pay for the $5,000 bill the mental health hospital had sent me. Medicaid would pay the hospital and for all my future outgoing therapy.

Anne became a support system for me. She offered to drive me to doctor's appointments. She called every now and then to see how I was doing. She was surprised that I had never done drugs. In fact, I had never seen drugs, not even marijuana. She said I could call her anytime. Anne became the bridge between the darkness I was stuck in and the light I so desperately wanted to see. She visited me when she was in my area. She took the time to ask if I needed anything. I knew I could call Anne if I ever needed anything. Most importantly, Anne always answered the phone.

Getting approved for Medicaid solved one problem: I was finally able to see a cardiologist after more than four years. Things got better. I saw a therapist once a week. Going to therapy gave me a chance to talk about my feelings.

My first session with a therapist was just a few days after I was discharged from the hospital. She was interested in what transpired in the weeks before I was hospitalized. There, I got to tell her about my past. We discussed family.

"I don't have any," I told her. I had Paul, but he was busy with his own life. He had his own struggles to overcome. We talked about my teenage years in America, the struggle I went through. The guilt I carried after I lost my mother. I struggled to understand why my father didn't love me. It was a good session. By the time the meeting ended, which was less than an hour, I felt a little better. I was glad to talk to someone who didn't judge me for any of my life decisions. Someone who understood my struggle with mental illness. Mostly someone who was in a position to help me professionally. She didn't think I needed medication. At least not yet. We would first try therapy without meds and see if things improved.

There was a sense of freedom in the therapist's office. It was a place where I could be myself. I could say anything I was feeling and no one would laugh at me or say I was crazy. I could even cry when talking became too overwhelming. It was my safe place.

I thought about going back to school. Most importantly, that cloud over my head was gone. The hammer wasn't smashing my heart anymore, and I was content for once. My life was similar to a roller-coaster, full of ups and downs.

Those three days in the hospital taught me a lot about life. I learned that things do get better; it just doesn't happen overnight. I learned that I was not alone and I wasn't crazy. There were so many people out there with the same problem. So many books had been written on depression. I wasn't the only person in the world dealing with the problem. Unlike people in my culture, the people in the hospital knew how I felt. They listened, they understood what I was going through, which meant more to me than a damn green card or all the money in the world. Now I knew what I needed to do to make things stay the way they were. I needed to make some changes in my life, rethink what I wanted to do, no matter how bad it hurt, and never stop until I got to where I wanted to be.

First, I was going to let go of everything that added to my stress. That included having a boyfriend and caring about people who didn't care about me. I reapplied for school but decided that I would attend as a part-time student. I wanted to stay away from anything that made my life more stressful, especially my so-called family. By then I no longer needed my parents' income tax return in order to qualify for financial aid.

The first semester I went back, I only took a yoga class; it helped me relax, plus it eased my way into the college environment. Once that semester ended, I started going to school nonstop, taking evening classes because I worked during the day. At the time, I was working at a call center, and I liked it. There were several people working in that office, at least twenty, some of whom were also Haitian. There were several rows with at least five seats each. I had my own cubicle where I hung my favorite Haitian calendar and a picture of my goddaughter, Sonya, on the wall. The center only took incoming calls from customers who were having issues with their EZ Pass. It was a laid-back environment. Most of the employees were nice. It was like being part of a mini family.

I used to start working at seven in the morning and worked until around 3:30 in the afternoon. I would then catch the local bus to another town where I started classes from six in the evening until 9 p.m. At first, I focused on English and math courses. There, I started making like-minded friends. Being around them gave me hope.

Paul had just started going out with Guerda, a girl who used to be my acquaintance. I hated their relationship. I hated it the same way he had hated my relationship with Pretty Boy. Guerda didn't like me, and I didn't like her. I was never sure why she didn't like me, but I didn't like her because I didn't think she loved my brother, and I didn't want him to get hurt.

"Guerda said you don't like her," he told me one day.

"Oh?"

I hadn't done anything to her, but now that I knew she was saying things behind my back, I was determined to show her that I didn't like her. It must have been close to midnight when we had a big argument about Guerda.

"Guerda's a bitch," I said in Haitian Creole.

"No, she's not," he said. "You're a bitch. You're just jealous because you can't keep a man."

I was heated. Paul was one of the few people that I admired, and he called me a bitch for a girl that he'd just met maybe a month or two earlier. I wanted to break the cordless phone on his head that night. I wanted to fight him and hurt him, but I was too hurt to do any of those things. My low self-esteem would not allow me to overlook what he said or forgive him. I felt like I was going to suffocate, the fact that he told me I couldn't find a good guy and I was jealous of Guerda. He was right. I had made some poor choices in guys. At twenty-four years old, I had not found the right one. I was still trying to find myself, for that matter.

I didn't hate Guerda; I hated the fact that she was taking Paul away from me. I'd always been able to count on Paul, and I hated that I was losing him. I'd lost my mom, my dad, Sheila, and I was going to lose Paul too, so I fought back. Although Sheila and I were talking, it was only once in a while, and she didn't really care about me as a person. Paul was right: I did have bad luck with guys, and no one wanted me—not even my own family.

I called Diana that night, telling her that I wanted to hurt Paul. I was crying to her how much I didn't want to see his face. Diana could hear the commotion in the background. She offered to pick me up that night, which she did. The Haitian lady we rented from thought I was kidding; she begged him to apologize and for me not to leave, but nothing could stop me. That night, I packed the few clothes that I owned and left. Paul and I didn't speak another word to each other. While I hated him, he had everything that he wanted—he was happy.

My job was a good thirty to forty-five minutes from Diana's house by bus, and I had to start work at seven in the morning, so I took the 5:30 bus every day. It didn't matter if the temperature was below zero or if there was a blizzard; I had to stand at that bus stop and wait for the bus to come. It was my loss if I chose not to wait, because I needed the money. Once I got off work, I had to hurry to take the next bus back to where I lived so I could get there on time for my 6:00 p.m. class. By then, there was only enough time to grab something to eat and go to class.

When I took English 101 at the community college, I remember that I was the only Black woman in the class. It never bothered me because I knew why I was going there. I never tried to make any friends in English class. I always sat in the last row, where I could be alone and focus. However, I did make some friends in my math class because it was more diverse. Although I had been in America for nearly ten years by then, I had spent most of my time around other Haitians. There were times when I was tired, hungry, and ready to quit. Still, I promised myself that it was a sacrifice that I would have to make only for a little while, and then everything would be better.

There was one day when the class was discussing race and education. I took the opportunity to tell the professor how my cousin Mark was considered gifted because he scored so high on an assessment test. Their next-door neighbor, whose daughter went to the same elementary school, told my aunt that my cousin's test was different from her daughter's because he was non-white. I wasn't sure how much truth there was to the lady's statement, but it was a way to show that my cousin only looked gifted because he took an easier test. I could not believe the answer that came out of one girl's mouth.

"The only reason they do that is so Black people don't feel left behind. They want to make it easier on them," she said.

That was one of the most ridiculous things I had ever heard, and I felt like slapping her, but I didn't. The professor made me feel better by telling her that although I was the only Black woman in the class, I was also one of the best students in the class, so we could not measure intelligence by race. It felt so great to be a student once again. I couldn't say that my life was finally complete, but my heart was not so empty anymore.

There were times when I wished I could get a hug or just hear someone say, "I'm proud of you," but that never happened. Still, I didn't stop. I knew when to file my financial aid papers, I knew I didn't have any money or anyone else to help me pay for my tuition, so I did whatever I was asked to do, no questions asked.

Spring came, and I was doing great in school. Things were going too smoothly for me, and I knew something bad was going to happen soon—that's the way it'd always been. After living with Diana for three months, I realized that she had helped me enough; it was time again for me to move—this time on my own.

Although I knew the move was the best thing for me at the time, it was tearing my heart apart. Leaving Sonya was one of the hardest things I had to do because she was the one thing that kept me going most of the time. The little girl stole my heart the first time I laid eyes on her; it was almost like I'd given birth to her myself. Who was going to provide me with a big kiss and hug at the door if I didn't live with her anymore? Whenever I walked through the door and didn't kiss her, she always opened her arms and said, "kiss." Every night before she went to bed, she came to my room and kissed me goodnight. I had never seen another child like her—she was such a blessing to my soul, and sometimes I couldn't even believe that someone like her existed on this planet. Who was going to get my sandals for me or remind me to play my answering machine?

"Let's go get the mail," she told me every day when I got home, and she never forgot to hop on my back for the ride. I remember the night I had to move into my own place. She came into my room as usual, and I somehow felt obligated to tell her that I was going to leave. I couldn't help the tears from running down my face as I hugged and kissed her goodbye. She didn't understand that she was not going to see me anymore, so she followed me everywhere in the house that night and was particularly excited when I gave her the Barbie dolls that her mom had hidden from her in my closet. I gave all of them to her as a departure gift, and that put a smile on her face.

As I left, I was still asking myself how I would manage to see that child again. It was almost like I was her parent or something, and I owed it to her to be a part of her life. I needed her to know that I loved her, and I was going to be there for her no matter what.

Everything would get better over time, I thought.

I rented a room from a couple. It was a two-bedroom apartment where they lived with their toddler son. I rented the smallest room for $325 a month. My new place was kind of lonely, but it was peaceful, which was exactly what I needed. The room measured no more than ninety square feet. I slept on the floor until I had enough money to buy a bed. I ended up buying a full-sized bed for around $150 within a month. I did not own any other furniture. There was no money to buy a television. There was no desk for me to do my school work.

A month later, I managed to buy a used 1984 Plymouth sedan for five hundred dollars with my income tax refund. My new car ran great, except for the fact that I needed to hold my foot on the gas for a few minutes after starting it—otherwise, it would turn off. The ceiling was also rusty, so I could never touch it, otherwise my hands would be full of rusted powder. The seats were comfortable. Since it was a large car, it also cost me about twenty dollars in gas a week.

I changed jobs and started working as a receptionist for a small carpet cleaning company located in the next city where I made about $750 a month. I was the only person who worked in the office from noon until 5 p.m. The lady who opened the office left at noon. Customers did not really visit the office unless they were dropping off a rug for cleaning. The office was located in a house. There was a huge desk in a big room which would have been the living room. There, I would sit and answer the phone. My job mainly consisted of making appointments and confirming them. I also collected money from the guys at the end of the day. I would then prepare a deposit slip and take the money to the bank the following day.

Another older lady worked a couple days a week as a bookkeeper. She and I worked the same hours on the days that she was there. I enjoyed talking to her. She treated me like one of her grandchildren, and so did her husband. It was not a lot of money, but it was progress. I still had Medicaid, and by then, I had gotten a primary care physician. In addition to being able to see a cardiologist, Medicaid allowed me to see other specialists like a gynecologist.

I also did inventory part-time for a company where I worked as early as four in the morning whenever I could to help take care of myself. My job as an inventory specialist consisted of scanning merchandise so stores would know the number of items they had left. I had to drive to a new place for each job which was not good for my almost twenty-year-old car. I used the money I made for rent, food, car insurance, and clothes whenever I could. Without my second part-time job, I would have been short money for my monthly expenses.

One day on my way to work, I attempted to stop at a stop sign when my car proceeded to move forward. The car's brake felt floppy. It went down all the way to the floorboard of the car. Thankfully, there were no other cars around me, otherwise, I would have been in an accident. I didn't have any money to get the car fixed because I was barely making ends meet. That morning, a Good Samaritan called for a local mechanic to come get my car. They towed the car and the mechanic determined that my brake fluid was empty. The hose had been cut. He didn't say if it was due to the fact that my car was nearly twenty years old or if someone had done it on purpose. He charged me forty dollars to fix it.

I woke up one morning to find that my car window had been broken. Who could have done such a thing to me? I was barely making ends meet. Why would someone try to hurt me directly or indirectly? Now I had to fix the window but had no money, just more stress added to my senseless life. So, I told my friend Judith what had happened. She was my former co-worker from the call center, and she'd become a great friend. She agreed to lend me the money, but never took it back. I guess she felt sorry for me because we were the same age, but she lived with her parents, had her own room, and didn't have to pay bills as I did.

For once in my life, I felt like I had everything I needed and absolutely no one to give me stress. Besides, I didn't have time for anyone; I was always too busy. I left my house as early as 4:00 a.m. when I had to do inventory, left work at the cleaning company around 5:00 p.m., and went straight to school, which started at 6:00 p.m. with no time in between to even get some-thing to eat. Sometimes, I did have the time to eat, but I saved the money for living expenses. It was never enough; I always seemed to be missing at least five dollars a month for a bill. I shopped for no more than fifty dollars of groceries a month, and it always lasted. I was able to go to the grocery store and buy ten plantains for one dollar—that was ten whole meals. A pot of rice and beans could last almost a week because I was the only one eating it. There was never enough money for dairy, fruit, or vegetables, however, which led to severe constipation.

One morning as I was getting ready to go to work, my car refused to start. Maybe I needed a new starter, I thought. The same mechanic towed my car and determined that I had engine issues. It would cost over $400 to fix it, but I did not have that kind of money to spend on an old car. Since I was going to school and I received a refund from my Pell Grants, I was able to buy a new car that was listed on Craigslist for $600. My new car was a used 1989 Dodge Aries. It was burgundy. My new car looked a lot nicer than the old one, and I didn't have to keep my foot on the gas for a few minutes to warm it up. However, almost immediately I noticed some issues. Almost every time I stopped at a red light or a stop sign, the car would shut off. To prevent the car from shutting off, I had to ride my brakes so it would seem like the car was still moving. This caused issues for me because there wasn't always room for me to ride my brakes, especially if the red light was too long. Whenever the car turned off, I would simply restart it, and it would run again.

One day while I was driving, my car turned off. This time, the car would not turn on again. It was embarrassing. I didn't have a cellphone. Cars started honking and going around me with frustration. I did not know what to do. I was a bit scared. An older guy stopped to help me. I was only a few blocks away from the mall. He pushed my car so I could get it on the side of the road and then offered to give me a ride. I was terrified. Could I trust this man? What if he kidnapped me and killed me? There were not many people I could call for help. I decided to accept a ride to the mall. The man drove a Porsche. I sat in the front seat, looking scared. He unlocked the doors and lowered the windows to put me at ease. I appreciated that.

Then he said, "How old are you? Nineteen?" I didn't even have time to answer when he said, "Don't worry, I have a daughter your age." He dropped me off at the mall where I caught the bus to a church member's house to get help. Although I was not a regular church member in Salem, I still attended service every now and then. That church member drove me back to where I had left the car and had it towed to his mechanic. He said I didn't have to worry about paying for it. What a blessing it was.

I remember driving Diana's car one day to work. My car was in the shop, so I borrowed hers. Right after I dropped her off, I realized that her tire was flat, so I stopped at a gas station near her job to put some air in it. Her sister, Rachelle, was in the car that day, and she noticed it too. I'd driven less than a block before realizing it. By the time I got off from work, the tire was already too flat, and I couldn't drive it anymore. I went straight to a gas station right next to my job, where they put a new tire on for $65. When I told Diana that night, she said there was a new tire in the car that I could have used, but I did not see it. Neither did the shop employees. She offered to pay me back. I agreed because I really needed the cash to pay the bills. Rachelle later told me that Diana wasn't planning to pay me back because her boyfriend, Oliver, had told her not to.

I thought that was weird because she offered to pay me back, and I didn't even ask her. I decided to test her—to ask her for the money to see if what Rachelle said was correct. I brought it up a week later.

"I don't owe you anything," she said. "You drove it. You messed it up, so you fixed it." Then she walked away. Did I mention the flat happened less than one block after I dropped her off at work? It did.

Rachelle blamed Oliver for Diana's behavior, but I didn't believe any man could make a woman do anything that she didn't want to do in the first place. We all had the right to choose, and she'd made her choice.

"Fine, I make money, money doesn't make me," I said to her before I left. But that meant not being able to pay for my car insurance that month, which cost around $80.

I had to move again, and I'd used all my money to move into my new place. I rented another room from a couple with a teenage son. My new room came with its own bathroom, which was great. It was almost like having my own studio, except I had to share a kitchen with them. The room came with a small refrigerator, which felt amazing. I did have a television this time—it was probably a thirty-inch television. I found it in the trash next to my home. It didn't have any sound, but I could see pictures which was better than nothing. I also managed to buy a desk to do my school work. Things were really improving for me.

Without the $65, I had no money for my car insurance. It was going to expire in a few days, and Diana knew it. I was pissed, but it was my fault, as I should've never borrowed her car. But she used to borrow my car too, so I had no reason to feel guilty.

I drove the car to work and school with no insurance until Rachelle offered to lend me eighty dollars to pay for the insurance. I promised to pay her back, which I did as soon as I got my paycheck. I look back at my life after that incident, and although things looked better, they were still not going the way I wanted them to. I worked, but could barely buy myself the things that I needed. It was always a struggle to pay my rent and car insurance. Only school was going great.

Johnny relocated to the West Coast with his family, where he worked in his dad's landscaping business, so I didn't have anyone to talk to any longer. At least not as often as I would have liked to. I mean, he called me whenever he could, but it wasn't the same.

I remember one month I was missing money to pay my rent; I needed $70. I was going to get paid about three days after it was due, but I could not be late because there would've been a charge that I could not afford to pay. I asked everyone that I knew, including members of my family, but no one had money; they all claimed to be broke. As hard as it was for me to do, I even swallowed my pride and asked Micho, but the only money he had in the bank was the minimum amount to prevent him from getting hit with a fee.

Even though Nadia helped with my financial aid application, I still didn't have much contact with her. She wasn't considered an enemy, but she was not my friend either. I fed her with a long spoon. One more time, Judith saved me, she didn't take the money when I offered to pay her back, and I was grateful to her. I didn't want to go back, I needed to go forward, so I talked to Rachelle about transferring to the four-year college that she was attending at the time. I needed to surround myself with people who were moving forward with their lives. I needed people to tell me what worked for them so I could try it. My goal was to get out of poverty and depression, and getting a degree was going to be my ticket out.

"It's a great idea. I'll tell you everything you need to do to get in," Rachelle told me.

I was willing to do anything she said, so I closed my mouth and opened my ears. I applied to the school and started providing documents such as my transcript from the community college. The bookkeeper from work and her husband looked over my college entrance essay. I still remember the day I received my acceptance letter. Because of my income, I was also qualified for the full Pell Grant amount the federal government was offering for low-income students. I felt normal. I felt like any other young person out there. I was almost free.

I could see a tiny light from afar. All I had to do was walk toward it. Rachelle warned me about the possibility of not finishing college and ending up in a worse position. I was about to give up the room I rented for a room in the dorm at school. I donated my car to a breast cancer charity. I gave my bed and my desk to a neighbor. My television went back to the trash where it belonged. What would happen to me if I dropped out of college? Where would I go? Who would take me in until I get on my feet? Paul and I were still not talking. Sheila and I rarely talked. My relationship with my dad was nonexistent. Failure was not an option; I had to go nonstop and come out on the other side a different person.

CHAPTER 16

HEADING TO UNIVERSITY

On August 25, 2002, I took the bus to a four-year college in North Adams, which was located about three hours from my house by car. However, the bus ride would take much longer than that. I started my journey to the university with two suitcases and a blue duffle bag with my radio and shoes inside. Rachelle also took the bus with me since she was already a student there. I got such a sweet feeling on the bus; almost everyone seemed to be a student. Most of them were going back to school. I felt so special that morning, as if I was worth something. I felt like life finally had something to offer me. I didn't want to die anymore, I had a bright future waiting for me, and it was up to me to make it happen. Most of the students on the bus seemed to be in their teens, but I looked young, so it didn't matter how old I was. No one could tell.

After we got off the bus ride, which took at least six hours, we caught a taxi to the school. There, I saw so many cars with parents dropping their kids off for school, and at least ninety-five percent of those students were white. There were also Black students getting dropped off by their parents, but they were few. The students on my bus were mostly nonwhite, especially immigrants. It didn't matter though that I had no family to drop me off—the point was that I was on my way to success.

When I got to the dorm that day, it felt weird. I was part of a group of people who were considered normal. I was far from normal. There was nothing normal about wanting to end one's life. It was not normal to cry for no reason. It was not normal to be homeless. It was not normal to be hungry. It was not normal to hurt all the time. It almost felt like I didn't belong there. A place like that dorm was too good for people like me, a poor Haitian girl who spent the first fourteen years of her life living in a one-room house in Haiti. A girl who could not speak a word of English a few years earlier. A girl who had been through Hell and back. That day, I felt like a human being again.

My room was in a suite with two other rooms, but I got the biggest room by luck. Meghan and Sophia shared the first room on the right. Another girl stayed in another room by herself. She mostly kept to herself so we didn't spend much time with her. I never really got to know her on a personal level. I shared the biggest room with Victoria. Our suite had a large bathroom with two stalls and two showers. There were at least two or three sinks for us to brush our teeth. The suite also had an open area that looked like a family room. It had two sofas and a small television. My room had two over-sized twin size beds. My bed was away from the door. There were two closets and two desks.

I did not have a computer, so I mostly used my desk to study and used the computer lab for work that required me to type papers or do research. I liked it. It was completely different from what I was used to. I had purchased a meal plan for nearly $2,000 for the entire semester. I would never be hungry again and would always know where my next meal was coming from. Financial aid and student loans had covered my tuition and room and board for the school year. It was the most stable I had been in a long time. That was the first time I felt safe in a very long time. The dorm room had cable, which meant I could watch movies and shows.

There I met my roommate, Victoria, and suitemates, Meghan and Sophia. Victoria was an exchange student from China who spoke English beautifully; I could not even believe that she was not an American. Victoria was her English name. Mei was her Chinese name. Meghan and Sophia were white Americans from outside Boston. At first, Sophia didn't talk to me much; she was not very comfortable around Black people, which she later admitted to me. Meghan was a little friendlier; she said hi to me at least ten times in an hour like I was deaf or something. I had to tell her that my memory was working correctly, and I did remember that she'd already said hi.

"I was just trying to be nice," she said.

North Adams was a small town northwest of Salem. Although I had always lived in the suburbs, North Adams was the smallest city I had ever lived in. Most of the residents were Caucasians, with very few Black residents. I enjoyed living there.

It wasn't long before I adapted to the new area; besides, it wasn't like I had a home to miss. I started taking classes toward my business degree. My first semester, I took twelve credits. Since I did not have to work many hours a day and go to school, I had plenty of time to get my work done. I enjoyed being able to walk to the dining hall to eat food that someone else had prepared. All I had to do was swipe my student identification card and I could eat. The school had several locations to eat, but the main dining hall was similar to an all-you-can-eat buffet. I loved the stir-fried rice from the Asian section. Staying on campus allowed me to eat better. Something as simple as cereal and milk, which had been a luxury to me, was now the norm. I could eat a banana every day. I could eat as many fruits as I wanted to. I could have scrambled eggs for breakfast. I could even see the campus doctor whenever I didn't feel well.

Life was good for a while. Everyone else was homesick. Victoria would whine the whole day about missing her home and family. Sophia and Meghan would speak to their parents daily and couldn't wait for a break to go home. Of course, I never said anything. I didn't have a home. I didn't have a family to call or call me, and a break was not going to make a difference to me because, as far as I was concerned, the dormitory was my new and only home. This new place was my Heaven. A beautiful and peaceful one too.

"Don't you miss home? Don't you miss your family? How come you never talk about home?" the three of them would ask.

I had no one to impress; besides, I was there to educate and better myself, not to show off what I had or missed. The clothes in my suitcases were all I had anyway. The dorm was my home, even though to some, it was only a temporary place to study. I could see that it was just a place for some of them to pass time, but it was a luxury for me. For the first time in years, I felt safe.

I didn't have to worry about paying my rent every month or being homeless; I didn't have to work nine hours a day and still be unable to pay my bills. I got to eat better, and whenever I wanted to, not having to rely on a fifty-dollar monthly grocery budget. A lady even cleaned the bathroom and suite every day, so my only responsibility was to get good grades.

"I don't have a home, I don't have a family, and I don't miss anything," I said.

"You're so funny," Meghan said to me.

Soon they understood that I was not kidding because when the first Thanksgiving break came, I was the only person who would be left in that suite.

"Don't you want to see your family?" Victoria asked.

"I don't have one," I replied. It was the truth. I didn't have a family. The dorm had been my safest home since I left Haiti and Martin's home.

Still, Victoria thought I was kidding until the day she left for China. It wasn't like I didn't want to go somewhere or see anyone; I didn't have any place to go. It had already been many years since I'd left my father's house. He knew I was going away for school but never said I was welcome in his house, so I wasn't going to invite myself. I have to admit, as rough as my heart was, it still hurt to see my roommate speak to her mom on the phone every day. It hurt to hear Meghan say how she couldn't wait to eat her mom's pies, and for Sophia to say how she couldn't wait to be in her comfortable bed at home. I envied all of them, but not in a bad way. I don't think I wanted what they had, but my life was abnormal in my eyes.

It's funny how we're never satisfied with anything we have. My biggest dream came true: I was going to school, something that I had always wanted, and yet I still wanted more. I wanted a family, someone to ask me how classes were going, and whether I was getting good grades. I needed someone to ask me if I ate, if I was happy, to give me a hug sometimes, just someone to tell me that things were going to be okay. They never came, so I went on without any of them. I guess that's what motivated me the most when the girls watched a nice movie or show on television. I was studying or reading. I was doing anything to keep myself busy. As an immigrant who had to learn English and had to struggle with life, I had to work ten times harder than my roommates who had very good educational backgrounds.

I knew I had to work extra hard because I couldn't afford to fail and get kicked out of school. If that happened, then my life was over. Soon I started to feel empty again, and everything the girls did got on my nerves, starting with Victoria speaking Chinese on the phone, to Meghan telling me how she missed her mom, to Sophia telling me how she couldn't wait to rearrange her bathroom at home. I didn't want to be around them anymore. I started avoiding them by spending more time in the TV room, although I wasn't watching anything. I wanted to be away from happy people. The more time I spent with them, the more I realized how much I didn't have. They always wanted to do something fun, like going to see a movie or just having dinner out when they were tired of the dining hall food.

Victoria's parents deposited money in her bank account regularly, and so did Meghan's. Sophia also got a check from her family every month; she was the only one out of the four of us with a car. On the other hand, I couldn't do anything fun that required money, and everything in that town required money. I mean, if it were summer, it would be a different story. I could go hiking. But in the winter, I didn't see much to do without money. I'd arrived at the school with $300, but my bank account was now depleted, because I'd used the money for necessities—woman stuff.

"How much money do you have in your bank account?" Meghan once asked since I never went out. She thought I had so much money saved in the bank, and I was just trying to be cheap. I don't think I had more than ninety dollars in the bank that day, and I had a few more weeks left before the semester ended. I hated the dining hall food as much as they did, but I didn't have any other choice. I mean, it was better than eating boiled plantains and rice every day.

It was time for Thanksgiving break, and the residence hall was going to be closed, and I'd have to pay eight dollars a day to stay in my room. Diana asked if I wanted to come to her house for Thanksgiving and to have a break from school, so I bought a bus ticket for fifty dollars. Thanksgiving with Diana was fun. She always made a big roasted turkey. I was so happy to see Sonya. She was almost five years old at the time. Diana's boyfriend, Oliver, made mashed potatoes. Rachelle made some rice and beans, and I made the sauce. It felt nice to be among friends. I did not visit my dad that Thanksgiving break. It wasn't any of his business. He did not care about me.

When I returned to the school that Sunday afternoon, Meghan, Sophia, Victoria, and I went straight to the dining hall for dinner. The school served the usual. There was a burger and fries section, an Asian section, a pasta section, and a pizza section. Every now and then, they served some chicken wings with barbecue sauce. Those were usually my favorites.

Everyone was talking about their break from school. Meghan spoke about her mom's cranberry sauce that went well with the turkey. Sophia spoke about her beautiful bathroom and huge room at home. Victoria talked about her pleasant experience at her cousin's house in New Jersey and how she could not wait to visit again. I, on the other hand, had nothing to talk about.

"Were you happy to see your family?" Meghan asked.

"I don't have any family," I replied.

"You're so funny," she said at the table.

As much as I felt out of place half the time, I also appreciated the fact that they saw me as their equal. At times, it made me feel normal; I was one of them, at least on the outside. Now, they all started to get on my nerves. I just wished we could've talked about something else like school or just us, but no home or family. That Thanksgiving weekend, I'd slept in the living room of Diana's house, and I'd stayed out most of the day. I mean, I was happy to see Sonya, but it wasn't my home, and it was not any of my friends' business to keep me occupied.

Final exams started a little over a week later, and I thanked God that I had the strength to study. Winter vacation was great, at least better than the dorm. I spent the entire holiday in Atlanta with Martin and Sheila. Martin had offered to pay for my train ticket, which was a blessing. By then, Sheila and I were talking a little more.

There, I was treated like a princess, at least for the first day. Martin was happy to see me. He took me out to eat at a local Haitian restaurant. Sheila showed me her new place. She let me borrow her car. A few days into the trip, everyone expected me to make myself at home, so no more special treatment.

My relationship with Sheila was a love-hate relationship. She had established a life for herself in Atlanta without me, and I had established my life without her. I still had not forgiven her for how we split up after my mother died. There was a wall between us. It was like we were both walking on eggshells, trying not to hurt the other's feelings. I did not trust her one bit, and I don't think she trusted me or even liked me.

Soon, I received my first report card, and I was happy to see that I had passed all my classes with mostly As and Bs.

I didn't like sleeping at other people's homes. There's a type of respect required when one stays at someone's house; plus, different people run their homes differently, so I was always afraid of breaking the rules and coming off as disrespectful. I had no other choice but to spend that time in Georgia; however, my next option was a shelter because I could not afford to stay in the dorm. I stayed in Georgia for at least one month.

On my way back to Massachusetts, I met a guy on the train. His name was Sean. The train had stopped to pick up passengers when I spotted a tall, brown-skinned guy at the station, one of the most handsome guys I'd ever seen in my life. I wished for him to get on the train, and he did. Next thing I knew, he was standing next to me.

"Is this seat taken?" he asked.

"No, no, no," I replied.

I was so excited that he would sit next to me that I moved my stuff from the seat in a rush. He smiled. We talked half the night about Haiti. He seemed to think that I could tell him everything he needed to know about voodoo because I was Haitian. We talked about what we wanted in the future and how many kids we wanted to have (not with each other). I told him I wanted to name my daughter Melissa and my son Sean, and he laughed. I didn't know why at first, but I later found out that his name was Sean, so he found it funny.

It was time for me to go to sleep, but I could not sleep sitting up. Sean offered to have me sleep on his lap. I didn't accept his offer because I didn't know him that well, but I found myself sleeping against him the next morning. He was still sleeping when I woke up, so I'm not sure if he knew I'd been asleep on his chest. I wanted to keep in touch with him, but I didn't want to sound pushy. I left my car to talk to a Dominican girl in another car for about an hour. When I got back, he was already gone. I wish that I had asked for his number. Not that I wanted to date him, but I thought he was a nice person.

I returned to school for my second semester. This one was going to be the hardest because I was running out of money. I applied for all the available jobs on campus, but no one called me, not a single one. Martin gave me $200 on my way back to Massachusetts, but that money could not last me a whole semester. Since I'd worked the previous year, I had a refund check from the Internal Revenue Service for $250.

The second semester was a bit lonelier than the first. Victoria had moved back to China. Sharing a room with her did not have too many issues since she didn't party or drink. I was afraid of who my next roommate would be, so before the first semester ended, I requested that I get my own room. In order to be approved, I had to give a medical reason. I went to the campus physician and asked that I get a waiver to get my own room due to asthma. The waiver was approved. I stayed in the same room except now I had two of everything. I moved my bed closer to the other bed where Victoria used to sleep and turned them into one large king-sized bed. I used one desk to do school work and the other one to hold my products such as shampoo and deodorant.

One evening, I decided to stay in my room. As happy as I was with the way my life was going, depression still snuck up on me every now and then. I didn't always have the energy to hear my new friends talk to their parents and siblings over the phone. They reminded me too much of what I was missing. That evening, I stayed in and didn't want to talk to anyone. Meghan knocked on my door and asked if she could come in, but I didn't answer. I had been carrying a picture of my mom in my wallet since she died. It was the closest I would ever get to her. I knelt in front of my bed with a picture of my mother and cried. I cried until I had no more tears to shed. I asked God, "Why?" I needed her so much for emotional comfort. I cried myself to sleep that night. The next day, Meghan asked if everything was okay. I told her a little bit of what I was feeling.

"You're the most miserable person I know," she said. *Whatever*, I thought. Who cares what she thought? She probably could not survive one day in my shoes.

The end of the semester came, and I had to find an off-campus house because financial aid did not cover the summer term. Staying on campus for the summer was not an option. Most people left to go home. Very few students stayed in town, mostly because they were international students.

I remember the day Meghan and Sophia left. Sophia's parents came first, and she was so happy to leave. Tears ran down my face that day, and Meghan thought it was because I was going to miss Sophia, but she got it all wrong. I just wished I had a home to go to that day.

When Meghan's parents came to get her, she hugged me goodbye and promised to call and send me gifts for the summer. By then, she knew that I didn't have a home; she finally believed me. Everyone was gone, and it was just me in the suite waiting for Sunday to move out. I had chicken noodle soup for those two days, using the small electric hot pot that Sophia had given me before leaving.

CHAPTER 17

NEW HOUSE OFF CAMPUS

Sunday came, and it was time to move into my new summer house. It was probably 1:00 in the afternoon when the cab dropped me off. There, I met my new roommates, Anthony and Soo-ah. Anthony was from Washington, D.C., and he was the type of guy who tried as much as possible to enjoy life to the fullest. Soo-ah was an international student from South Korea who got only the finest things in life. It wasn't long before Soo-ah and I clicked. Although I wasn't spoiled or rich, we had a lot in common.

The house was $500 for the entire summer, including a $200 deposit before I moved in. By that time, I had less than $250 in the bank. I used $200 for the rent, $10 for a taxi to move, and bought some food, including a forty-eight-pack of Top Ramen chicken noodle soup from Wal-Mart. When I was done shopping, I had $4 in the bank.

The first thing Soo-ah wanted to do was to go shopping for food. I told her I was too busy since I didn't have any money; I only had four dollars in my bank account. She must've asked me for an entire week, and I gave her the same excuse. I guess she got tired of asking because she went to the store alone and shopped. She later told me to feel free to take anything from the fridge. Of course, I didn't. Besides, I had been telling her that I didn't have time to go shopping. I never told her I didn't have any money.

I ate my chicken noodle soup three times a day for almost two weeks until I couldn't smell it anymore. I thought of everything to get some money, but I couldn't come up with any answers. I took summer courses covered by student loans, and I was supposed to get a refund check. Until I got a job, the loans were the only thing that would keep me off the streets. However, it was going to be another month before the bank send the money.

When I attended class that week, the professor said we needed to buy a book for $23. My heart was pounding because I didn't have the book, and I certainly didn't have the money to buy it. I was so desperate that I thought of calling my dad for money, but I decided not to because I knew he wouldn't help me. I called a lady that I had been friends with for about four years, and I asked her for $10. She couldn't help me either. I applied for work-study that summer and was approved, but could not get a job on campus because I was too late.

It was strange how I never felt depressed during that entire time. I forced myself to eat that soup even when I couldn't look at it anymore. I could not even taste it, but I ate it to keep me going through the day. I had one last choice, my best friend, Diana. She wasn't perfect, but she was one hell of a friend. Her sister Rachelle picked up the phone when I called.

"Where's your sister?" I asked.

"She's not here," Rachelle answered.

I was desperate, so I got straight to the point. "I need some money. I have four dollars in the bank, and I've been eating chicken soup for the past two weeks," I told her.

Rachelle explained how Diana didn't have any money, but since she had been in my shoes before, she knew how I felt and was going to pass the message on.

"I have a check here for $120," she also said. "I'll send you $50 today if you give me your account number."

She told her sister, and they deposited a total of $100 in my bank account that same day, which I used the next day to buy food.

So, I asked myself if blood was really thicker than water. When I was growing up, that's what I was told, that family was better than friends, but family had turned its back on me while friends had stuck around through thick and thin. Micho was a lost cause—I knew I couldn't count on him for anything. Paul and I were not talking at all. From what I heard, he was still dating Guerda. Sheila and I rarely talked. We never fully recovered from that split after my mother died. She had made new friends and they became her family. She called their mother "Mom." She called them "sister" and she called their children her "babies."

Well, I managed to survive on my own somehow. I remember being so desperate for money that summer that I volunteered to be part of an experiment for asthma patients at a local clinic.

The last thing I wanted to do was to be a dummy for science. Still, I needed the money so much, and, to me, trying their new inhaler was much better than prostitution. I also managed to pass my class. My original grade was an F, but the professor had pity on me. She was shocked when I told her I didn't have the $23 necessary to purchase the book. So, after failing the final exam, she agreed to give me one last chance to retake the exam at home by using information from the internet only. I passed. That professor made me realize that there were still good people in this world and that God was still looking out for me.

That summer went great, except for the people who visited my roommate, Anthony, regularly; they were the noisiest people I'd ever met in my entire life. There was music in the house from the time they got there until six the next morning most of the time. I could not sleep unless they were sleeping. Anthony was nice, though. He always apologized whenever I got out of my room and stared at him.

As different as we were, I enjoyed speaking to him. We seemed to have more in common than I thought. He was struggling to make it, just like I was. We both had dads who didn't care about us, and I guess we both wanted to be happy. I had never been this close to an African-American before besides James, so I can honestly say that I learned a lot from him. I hadn't learned much from James other than there were mean people in this world, and Anthony taught me not to generalize. I learned a lot about what goes on in big cities. Although I had been alone and broke, I had always lived in the suburbs. I had always spent most of my time around other Haitians and immigrants. I sometimes judged people from the city because of what I heard of them, but now that I talked to Anthony, I understood where he was coming from, and I could relate to that somehow.

Anthony told me about the police stopping him and searching him for no reason. At times, they would even handcuff him while searching him. I realized I had been blind all this time. These things didn't happen in my town. My immigrant friends never told me such stories. He opened my eyes to a whole new world right inside America, a world I didn't know existed even though I had lived here for many years.

August came, and it was time again for school. The residence hall had gone up by $200, and I was unsure whether I was going to get a job on campus, so I weighed the option of moving off-campus. With the financial aid and the student loans that I received, I was able to stay in the same house and pay about $900 less than I would have spent on campus. I also didn't have to worry about buying a meal plan, which would have cost me a couple thousand dollars or more.

That summer, I found out that my friend, Ricardo, from middle school, was getting married to his long-time girlfriend. Ricardo, Diana, and I had met in middle school when we were all in the eighth grade. We'd somehow managed to stay in touch with the help of Diana; she was the glue that kept everything together, especially in my life. Ricardo was also Sonya's godfather. So, in the Haitian culture, Sonya would be a "godsister" to my kids and to Ricardo's.

The wedding was going to be on a Saturday afternoon, and I decided to go with Kurt, an American guy that I'd been talking to for months in a Yahoo chatroom. Kurt was one of the most handsome guys I had ever met. Some of my friends even thought he was "too handsome" and dressed too well. He was too cute, they said. I used to sit and admire his blonde, straight hair, his flawless skin, pink lips, and beautiful smile. Meeting Kurt for the first time was both exciting and scary. What if he was not who he said he was? What if he killed me? It was a chance I would have had to take to find out.

The day of the wedding, Kurt dressed up in a nice beige suit. At one point during the ceremony, he asked me why the bride was so much taller than the groom. We both laughed. After the ceremony, we stayed outside for most of the reception. We talked about our dreams and aspirations.

"What do you think of marriage?" he asked.

I told him that I would have liked to get married in about three years.

"I need six years," he blurted out. "How about children?"

I told him I would like to have two kids.

"Children are a waste of money," he said. "I don't want any kids."

Well, that should have been a sign that the relationship would never work, but I liked him, so I overlooked them as small issues that could be worked out later.

I guess I didn't feel jealous that my friend was getting married and I was still single because I had a handsome date. Kurt was a law student at a university in the Boston area, but he had very little knowledge of how the real world operated. It was almost like he was living in his small world, and anything that didn't fit in his way of life just did not exist to him. At first, I used to wonder why such a handsome and intelligent guy liked me in the first place. He once said of all the women he had met in his life, I was the first to have the right key to his heart.

It's funny how my friends told me not to trust the guy. He was too good to be true, one girl told me. I guess that's what attracted me to him the most: he was too perfect. Kurt was educated, handsome, a good listener, an excellent writer, and was willing to make me happy. I could never get enough of him over the phone or in person, and vice versa. That was until we started spending too much time together and started to see each other's true colors. He complained that I was too negative; I needed to be happier, see the good side of life. I, on the other hand, started to notice that he looked down on people who did not attend universities. In my opinion, he did not have much respect for other people's culture. I admired an educated man, but I had very little respect for a man who valued himself based on money and knowledge. All he ever talked about was how to get an advanced degree and make millions; it was never to help people in general. How could I have been so blind?

I had always been a wise woman, but I was fooled by this guy's good looks and didn't see the other side of him. So, he thought I was too negative, but what made me so cynical? It's funny that I even tried to be positive to make him happy, as if he were the only guy in the world for me.

"I'm going to help you," he said, and I was comfortable

with that, although I don't ever remember asking him to help make my life better.

"You're going to be someone new," he said.

It was the last weekend that we were going to see each other, and I was so excited to have been able to leave school. It was located in such a boring town. I was also happy to see Kurt since it had been a month since he visited. I guess he was glad to see me too, with all the hugs and kisses I received at the train station.

First of all, I hated the subway in the city, which was where he lived. There were too many trains down there. I complained too much about the smell of urine. The subway made me feel claustrophobic. I must have complained about everything under the sun that day.

Then there was the phone call he made to his female friend in the hotel room while I was in the shower. I trusted him, but it pissed me off that he went on with his conversation even after I stood there waiting for us to go eat. It had been at least nine hours since I had eaten. I guess it was too rude to say, "I'm hungry; can you call your friend later?"

We went to the restaurant, a lovely one, I have to admit, right in the heart of Boston. Kurt never walked with me without holding my hand, but this time he didn't take my hand. Once we were there, he took pleasure in listening to the conversation that the couples next to us were having. For the first ten minutes, he acted as if I was not even there. It was not long before I caught his attention, however, without my even realizing it.

The water the waiter brought me had a piece of lemon in it. "Excuse me, may I have another glass of water without lemon?" I asked.

Suddenly, it was almost like Kurt was ashamed of sitting at the table with me. I was not acting like the more refined, civilized people around us. I should have kept that water because if they'd given it to me like that, then that was the way it was supposed to be.

"There was nothing wrong with the water; you're just too negative," he said.

The rest of that weekend was a blur because everything I did bothered Kurt. I wanted to get away as fast as possible. I returned back to school a couple days later, and the next time Kurt called to say hello, he apologized for being unable to stay long—he'd gone to exercise and was drained. I didn't think anything of it until I went to bed that night and had a weird dream. I was walking on a bridge made of steel; there were many holes in it, and I could see the ocean below, dark and troubling. I was on a cellphone, talking to him, but the cellphone dropped and fell into the sea through one of the holes. I looked for the phone, but never did find it.

I called Kurt that morning because I believed that dreams could be warnings, and I wanted to know if he was okay.

"You're so negative, you can't drink your water with lemon, you hate the subway, and you don't want to be happy," Kurt kept saying. It felt like a knife to the heart.

I wanted to punch him, but he wasn't in front of me. "You need to be more positive," he kept saying. I had been working on myself for a few years, and I was finally working toward feeling better about myself, but it wasn't going to happen overnight. Kurt grew up in a family with his parents and siblings. He had been protected his entire life. How dare he judge me? He had no idea how far I had come to be where I was in that moment. That morning, I realized that there was no way I could ever make Kurt happy because I had too much baggage. The timing was off. I could not be who he wanted me to be. Not in my current state of mind. The last thing I wanted was to break up with him. I liked him very much. But I was not the right fit for his life. He saw the full half of the glass, and I saw the empty half.

"I think we should break up," I said.

I realized that I could not make him happy, and I did not want to try. I did not want to lose track of my life while trying to please another human being. I had nothing to gain; if we were going to be together, he would have to accept me for who I was. I felt like I was going to suffocate. I wanted so much for him to tell me that I was wrong and that we belonged together, but he kept telling me what he wanted from me, things that I could not deliver. So, he finally agreed with me, and we broke up. I believe that's what he wanted; he just didn't know how to say it.

That morning, I went to see Frank, one of my new roommates, and told him that Kurt and I had broken up. I was crying. My throat was tight, and someone had torn my heart apart again. I was shaking, and again I wanted to die, but this time I had too much to lose. I could not study, eat, or focus. I spent what felt like days in bed, sleeping. I don't even remember taking showers or getting up to eat. Crying was the last thing I did before I went to bed and the first thing I did when I woke up. I failed my mid-term exams, all of them. I don't think I could have made it through without Frank. He listened to me ramble about how I missed Kurt. Frank was such a good listener.

I didn't understand how someone could have so much influence over someone else's life. To make myself feel better, I decided to get away from school, away from my house, so I wouldn't have to look at Kurt's picture, but mostly away from the phone. I didn't want to sit there and wait for his phone calls that were not coming. I decided to rent a car and took a trip to New York City with three other students from India, two of them a couple.

I'm not sure what I was thinking when I took a trip with two love birds when I had just broken up with someone. They didn't know what had happened, of course, so there was no way they were going to try to be sensitive toward me. The more they hugged and kissed, the emptier I felt.

It took me a while to realize that it'd never been about Kurt; it was about me not loving myself. It was about me wanting someone to fill that empty hole inside my heart. It was me looking for love in all the wrong places. It took one month for Kurt to call me and ask how I was doing. He said he wanted to give me time to calm down. That evening, we talked on the phone for over an hour. We laughed as well. I still liked him. I still enjoyed hearing his voice. But I also knew he wasn't mine. He said he wished things hadn't ended the way they did. We decided it was best to be friends.

CHAPTER 18

VISITING HAITI

I was single all over again, and I loved it. My grades were getting better, and I was determined not to date anyone until I graduated from college. Sheila, Paul, and Micho didn't call, as usual; I don't think they knew how much I needed to hear from them half the time.

Paul was busy living his life with Guerda. Sheila was busy with her friends and their kids. Micho was busy with his wife and step-children. That December, I decided to go to Haiti for a few weeks. Since I was living off-campus, my expenses were lower than what they would have been if I had been living in the dorm. I bought a plane ticket for around $250. Since I was eligible for the full amount of Pell Grants and student loans, I used part of my refund from my student loans to pay for my plane ticket. I needed to find myself, but I needed to be closer to the person I was missing all along. I knew I was not going to see her; she did not even exist anymore. But in my mind, being where her body was, was close enough.

I overcame my fear of flying and got on my first flight since 9/11. At first, it was scary, but then I figured, *If I'm going to die, I'll just die.* The important thing was that I made peace with God. I don't think there was one empty seat on that plane. The Haitians could not wait to get to their homeland to celebrate our Independence Day, January 1st. They talked about how they looked forward to eating pumpkin soup; the elderly lady next to me even carried a frozen turkey in her luggage. Although I loved and enjoyed pumpkin soup, I had a funny feeling about the whole trip.

I was going for a different reason; I needed to find my soul. My mom once told me, "If you're ever about to lose yourself, go to the place where your umbilical cord was buried, and you'll find it." I'm not sure whether she'd, in fact, buried my umbilical cord, but I knew what she meant by that line. When the plane landed, it was a bittersweet feeling. Sweet, that I was home, and bitter, because nothing in that place was going to be able to take my emptiness away. That was the first time in more than five years, since my mom's funeral, that I had stepped foot in my homeland. I guess it was a different feeling because when I'd gone there for her funeral, I knew that at least her body was there. This time was different because she did not exist at all anymore.

It felt comforting to see all those Haitians staring at me like I was a piece of treasure. People were all over, begging to carry my suitcase. When I refused, they caught an attitude like I owed them money because I was from the United States. When I finally made it outside the airport, I was crazy, looking for my Aunt

Claudette. I remember she told me not to go outside entirely until she calls my name, so I followed her instructions. The streets of Port-au-Prince were too dangerous for me to stand outside with suitcases. I was so relieved when I heard a voice say, "Coucou," then I knew I was safe.

In the car, I got to eat Tasso (fried goat or beef), bannann peze (fried plantain), and akra (Taro fritters) with pikliz (shredded cabbage and carrots with lots of scotch bonnet pepper). I could not believe how free I felt on that poor Caribbean island.

There, I saw my family, got to eat at a table with other people I could relate to, and went out and did fun things as a family. I got to speak my native tongue, Creole, and I got to see people that I hadn't seen in a very long time. Some of my old friends had already traveled to the U.S. or Canada—and back. I got to eat food that I had not eaten in ages, but I felt loved most of all. For the first time in five years, I felt like I was not alone in the world. It was almost like someone had taken all my burdens away, and I could finally breathe.

I genuinely believe I found myself during those three weeks. Although Haiti was dangerous and people were dying, although we used an inverter and candles due to limited electricity, I felt like I belonged there with the other Haitians. I also realized that no matter how long I lived in the United States, I was always going to be one out of more than ten million Haitians living in this world. That was never going to change. Haiti also made me realize that I had taken so much for granted. It never occurred to me how lucky I was to have had food on my table every day, clean water to drink, and a roof over my head.

For some people, a life in the United States represented paradise. For others, like Aunt Claudette, living in Haiti was paradise. It didn't hit me until I went to the other side of town, where I saw a little boy no more than eight or nine years old sleeping in the dirty street. He wasn't dirty because he wanted to be; he was not on the sidewalk because he wanted to get fresh air—the sidewalk was his bed, and the clothes on his back were dirty because they were the only ones he had. I wondered where his mommy was, why he was so alone. What had happened to his family? I guess that's when it hit me how fortunate I had been to be able to take care of myself, even after my mom had passed.

And then, there was a grown man sleeping in an alley with flies all over him, dark like charcoal. At first, I thought he was dead. I wondered why he was not taken to a morgue—until he moved. It took me a few minutes to realize that it was not his skin color; it was dirt. That alley, that dirty ground, was his bed. Those flies were his only friends. Why didn't anyone care?

Why didn't anyone care? I had asked myself that question before, but it had always been about me. For the longest time, I'd wondered why no one cared about me, but in Haiti, I came to realize how selfish I had been. I was better off than this guy and the little boy who were sleeping on the sidewalk. I had friends in college; maybe they did not call often, but they took the time to call once in a while. Why was this man so bony? Was he sick? I answered those questions myself days later when I saw that same man eating from the garbage that lay on the sidewalk and taking a bath with the dirty running water. I thought I had it bad, but other people had it worse.

I returned from Haiti feeling like a completely new person. Just like my mom had told me, I found myself down there. I went back to school, feeling refreshed. I had just moved into a new apartment the week before leaving for winter break, and I decided to get a job to help pay some bills and support myself. I still could not get a regular job at the school, and I was not qualified for work-study, but the dining hall needed help.

Working there was stressful. I chose to work in the dishroom because I did not want to be dealing directly with the students. I was also ashamed of the uniform shirt, and I did not want my friends to see me cleaning tables. Occasionally I was asked to wipe tables or put utensils out for the students whenever someone called in sick or when we were short-staffed. The supervisor said she liked it when I cleaned the tables because she didn't have to re-check my work; the few times she did, everything seemed perfect.

By then, I was a junior, and the amount of work I had for school had increased. I was taking fifteen credits and working about fifteen hours a week, sometimes more. Although fifteen hours doesn't sound like a lot, there was enough schoolwork for me to study around the clock. Even four or five hours at work took away from what I could've been doing for a class. I lived at least fifteen minutes from the school, walking distance, and when I got off work at 10:00 p.m. or later, I had to walk home. Fifteen minutes could be pretty harsh when the weather was below zero. It might not be bad for some, but for someone who grew up on an island where it's always summer, it was Hell.

My housemates were two Caucasian girls from Maine. We weren't friends, but they never bothered me, and that was good enough for me. I was getting stressed; my junior year was a killer, I had to go to work, and of course, I received no words of encouragement.

I was at work one evening, and for some reason, my head started spinning. When I sat down to steady myself, I started thinking that I was killing myself to get so many things done, but I didn't know why. Who was I working so hard for? I had nothing to live for; it was just me in the world, no one else. I felt my throat getting tight as if I was going to cry, so I decided to punch out. When I asked the manager to let me go home early, she nodded yes. After all, I had always been a good employee; I was always at work on time and stayed late when they asked.

I used to leave my book bag in my friends' room since they lived in the dorm, close to the dining hall where I worked. Carmen and Elena were sisters from the Dominican Republic. Carmen had long, straight hair. She was light-skinned, slim, and walked like a model. On the other hand, Elena kept her curly hair short. She was a little bit darker than Carmen, voluptuous, and not into walking like a model; she was more relaxed. When I walked into their room, they both stared at me. It was too early for me to be off from work.

I grabbed my bag and headed for the door without saying a word, and when Elena tried to stop me, I wanted to hold it back, but I could not help it anymore. Tears flowed from my eyes. Elena cried that night; she was sensitive.

"What's wrong?" they both asked. I tried to explain, but the words could not come out of my mouth. It was almost like my throat was clogged. I wanted to tell them how much I was sick of life, of being alone. I wanted to say that I was empty, that my life was not worth living, that I didn't know what to do about those feelings, but I could not. They wouldn't understand, and even if I told them, they both had their parents around. Elena once told me that she was close to her dad and that she called him Papi. Their mom called them every chance she got.

I left the building that night, speechless. It was cold, but I didn't feel it. My jacket was open, and I took my hat off. The cold air that went through my hair made me feel free, as if someone had taken all my burdens away. I felt like I had no bills, no schoolwork, no past; I had nothing to live for. I was completely free. Still, I couldn't stop the tears from coming, and I kept thinking, *I need my mom.*

I must have repeated that hundreds of times, and the more I did, the more I cried. I needed someone to understand, I needed someone to tell me that they knew how I felt, but no one could, because no one was in my shoes. I could call my sister, but she had her best friend Sissy; that was her new sister. She wasn't a good listener anyway. I thought of calling Paul, but I couldn't because we still weren't speaking. We'd never made up since the argument over Guerda. What would I look like calling him to tell him how miserable my life was? Then I thought of something that happened on my trip to Haiti.

One day, while we all sat in the living room, I asked my cousins if they'd ever been depressed. They all gave me a funny, puzzled look.

"We have no reason to be depressed."

"Well, you guys live in a poor country and have no jobs," I said.

"Nope, we're happy," they replied.

The question had left them incredulous.

So, I thought to myself that they didn't know what it felt like to be depressed. They lived in one of the poorest countries in the world, attended schools that offered limited prospects, were unemployed, and still … they were happy. I'd been taken from Haiti so that I could have a better life. Now I wondered whether a green card had changed my life for good. Although I lived in a rich country, I was always broke—just like people living in Haiti. I imagined my life had I stayed in Haiti: I probably would not have had a job—unemployment was at an all-time high. With my mom gone, I would not have any money. But would I be happier than I was in the U.S.?

When I got to the house that night, I went straight to my room and looked around. I had a computer, a television, a lot of books, clothes, shoes, and a bed. I had all the things that I didn't need and none of the things that I did need. I'd seen Haitians take boats to Miami for a better life. Some knew no one here, and yet they took the chance and succeeded in America.

I'd come young, had a green card, lived with family, and yet things were not better. *I must be missing something*, I thought. They probably knew something that I didn't, and I had to find out what it was. My small room was too lonely, so I decided to go outside and sit on the steps, wondering. The cold air cleared my head, and I could think better. I knew I didn't want to die; tomorrow could be better, all I had to do was sleep it off, and it would all be over.

I saw Carmen coming down the street, looking at every single house on the block. She had forgotten my house number, and she later said she'd been searching for four blocks. Carmen didn't like to walk. She visited my house once because the taxi dropped us there; she always complained it was too cold. I knew why she had walked that night; she wanted to make sure I was okay.

I could not stop laughing when I saw Carmen walking, looking at every single house on the block to find me. It was a good thing I was sitting on the steps.

"Are you okay?" she asked.

"Yes, I am," I replied.

"Would you like to go for a walk? We could talk," she suggested.

I accepted because I had nothing better planned. By then, my throat was cleared and the tears had stopped running down my face, so I felt like I could pour my heart out to her. I told her about my mom's death for the first time—how she died. I told her about the funeral, who attended and who didn't, and, most of all, how much I missed her. I told Carmen I needed people to care; I had been empty for too long, and my heart could not handle it anymore. I told her how I used to want to die, but I didn't feel that way anymore. She suggested that I care about people who cared about me and ignore those who didn't, including family. She also listed herself among those who cared about me, so I laughed. She laughed, and I felt better. Elena approached me the next day, but I told her that I had already talked to Carmen.

Then I met Tanya, the girl who was going to have the most significant impact on my life in college. We had both gone to the school of business and taken classes together. We really started talking when Kurt and I broke up but didn't get close until I moved into the new house.

Tanya was from Chile, so she could speak Spanish. Since she was dark-skinned, it was really easy to fool people and tell them that she was Haitian. She always told me when someone was gossiping in Spanish. Tanya was the one person who reminded me of Johnny. There was something special about her; there was something about her listening skills. I just could not believe it. I always told her that she had a gwo bouda (big butt); she knew it too, since she always wore those tight jeans.

Tanya had a beautiful mind, a big heart, and a cute smile. Tanya became a shoulder for me to cry on. I called her whenever things went wrong, and no matter what it was, she was always the first to know.

I remember one particular morning when I had a negative balance in my bank account. I was no longer working in the dining hall. Although I did have family members, they didn't call me, so I wasn't about to call anyone and ask for $20. I called Tanya that morning, right before class. Tanya could not help me either that day, but she'd given me $15 on two separate occasions. I told her that I wasn't going to class. I wanted to be alone; I didn't care about school anymore. I was even thinking of dropping out and getting a full-time job. I started crying on the phone, and when I tried to hang up because she was going to be late for class, she didn't want me to. She wanted to hear whatever was bothering me.

So I told her, "I want my mom, I don't have any food, and I don't have anyone to call."

One of my housemates heard me. I guess she listened to the entire conversation because when I was on my way out of the door for class, she hugged me and told me that she was there if I needed to talk. She also told me about her experience and said that she understood. Although she was raised by her mom only, we had different experiences. It was bad enough not to have a dad who cared, but it was even worse when there was no mom to make the hurt go away.

So, I took Tanya's advice that day and went to class. Carmen gave me $5 to get rid of the negative balance in my bank account, and I swallowed my pride and told Sheila that I didn't have any food in my house. She sent me $100, and that food lasted until the semester ended, which was about six weeks. The semester ended, and it was time to move again.

CHAPTER 19

MOVING AGAIN

Summer came again, and I had to move for the third time. As usual, I was broke before moving into the house, so my friend, Isaiah, helped me move my stuff. He was one of my roommates from when I lived with Anthony and Frank. It was a good thing I didn't have to pay before I moved into the house. This time, I qualified for work-study and got a job in the dean's office right after the semester ended. I was not going to get a paycheck for another month, however, so I decided to take summer classes. That way, I could apply for loans and use the refund to pay for my rent. Isaiah also suggested that I apply for food stamps. At first, I thought, *never*, I would not apply for food stamps, but that was before I looked at the balance in my bank account and opened my refrigerator—both were empty.

When I got to the welfare office, I felt like I didn't belong there, like I was better than the others sitting there waiting for their numbers to be called. I wore a hat that day so no one would recognize me. I was ashamed of being there; I was ashamed of myself. When I got to the window, I told the lady that I had an emergency and I needed food stamps—in a low voice. She couldn't hear me, but I repeated it until she did. I got an appointment.

"Bring your bank statement, your lease, phone bill, pay stubs, school registration, and all that stuff," she said. It almost felt like I had to strip to get the okay. But I did what the employees said, and eventually, my application was approved. I needed them; they didn't need me. I was just another statistic in their book. Food stamps did help because I got to eat without asking myself where I was going to get the money. I did have a job where I made $6 an hour, but I could now use that money for other things like to shop for some new clothes and save money for books for the following semester. Food stamps also got me a discount on my monthly phone bill, which went from $30 to a manageable $10.

Still, no one asked how I was doing at school.

That summer, I decided to take a trip to New York with Carmen, Elena, and two other girls from campus. I must have been driving for two hours when it all suddenly felt like a dream. In the dream, the car was going left and right, really fast, and whenever I tried to press the brake, my foot found the accelerator instead. And then images started to dim, although I could still hear the noise of the tires. The girls were screaming my name, and I could feel the out-of-control car hitting things on the interstate. I didn't know which way I was facing anymore. And as I closed my eyes, I thought, *God, help me.*

When the car finally hit the median barrier one last time and stopped, my seatbelt pulled me back, and my eyes opened. I felt like I was far away because, at first, I didn't remember what had happened. When I looked across the streets, so many cars had stopped for us. One guy had his hands over his head; I don't know if he thought we had died.

Carmen sat next to me in the front seat, and the guy asked her not to move and told us that they had already called the police. I heard Elena say that her head hurt. The three of them could not stop hugging one another in the back. Elena kept asking me what had happened, but I could not stop shaking. I told them that we had to get out of the car because I could smell it. I had this ugly picture in my mind that the car was going to explode. I could not get out on my side because the door was jammed. When we got out of the car, it was so mangled that the guy could not believe that there'd been five people in the vehicle. Others crossed the street and kept looking at us, looking for bruises, but all five of us walked out without a scratch. The car was a mess; the front was gone, the back was crushed in, and both sides were damaged. We were blessed that day. All this time I was inside the car, all the turning and hitting, I thought it was flipping, but it was spinning. The police officer came and asked how we were doing. He wanted to call an ambulance; he could not believe that all five of us had been in that car.

"Where are you guys hurting?" he kept asking, but we all gave him the same answer.

"We're fine."

We told him we were going to New York City. He said we were about an hour to an hour and a half away; we needed to call someone to come and get us, but there was no one. I told him the back of my neck was numb. It didn't hurt, but I could not feel it. He gave us a ride to a bus station to take the bus to finish our trip. The car got towed. People could not stop staring at us in the back of the police car.

"Look, no handcuffs," Elena said to those staring. The officer's parents were also from the Dominican Republic, so they spent the entire time talking about fun stuff. I sat there, scared of the car speeding on the same highway where I had just crashed. What if the police car crashed with us in it? He was speeding more than I was; I was going the speed limit, and we had crashed. The car accident happened around two that afternoon, and we got to our destination around nine in the evening.

The next morning, we all woke up with stiff necks. Mine hurt more than the others, I guess, because I was the driver. That morning we all went to the emergency room to get checked out.

"You're fortunate," the doctor said to me. "You have no broken bones. I have prescribed some pills for the pain."

But I was okay. At that time, I felt like I was given a second chance. When I told Tanya about the accident, she thought it was funny at first until a small ball started growing in the back of my head a week later. I started getting terrible headaches.

School reopened, and I was determined to ace my classes, at least that was what I told myself. I never understood why I was so unhappy. I saw students who would go through a year, looking forward to summer vacation. It never made a difference to me because December ended the same way January started. There was still a hole in my heart that I could not get rid of. I didn't understand why I was always so empty, why I cried so much and didn't want to be around people at times.

I visited the school's physician because of constant headaches, and she referred me to the school's therapist. I needed answers, so I agreed to see the therapist. The school charged around $120 to all students who didn't have personal health insurance. I had seen the school's physician a few times for common colds and flu, but I had never been to their mental health department before. I didn't know it even existed.

I remember the morning I wanted my life to be erased from this world. The director, who was also a psychiatrist, was standing a few feet from the receptionist when I showed up without an appointment. I didn't want them to know that I had been crying, but my voice gave me away.

"I need to talk to someone," I said. The director asked the receptionist to give me an appointment with him on the same day.

"Can you come back in a couple of hours?" she asked.

"I don't have two hours," I replied.

At that moment, I was in so much pain emotionally that one more minute felt like an eternity. I was not sure how I would go through the next two hours in that state of mind. I was in agony, and I needed something or someone to take that pain away.

The therapist saw me immediately. I wasn't sure how this shrink was going to take my pain away, but I wanted to try. I had nothing to lose and everything to gain.

When I went inside his office that morning, the first thing I did was cry. I just kept crying. I don't think I knew why I was crying so much; it felt so good to do so.

"Why are you crying?" he asked, right after he gave me some water and tissue.

"I don't know," I said. And I was being honest. I had no idea why I was crying. All I knew was I was really sad, and I felt like everything around me was dark.

So, he asked about my family's history, whether anyone in my family had been depressed before, and some other stuff. I could not really answer this question because depression was never discussed in my family. It wasn't accepted as an illness in my culture, which was why no one understood what I was going through all those years. I am not even sure if my mother dealt with depression because she kept so much inside. He wanted to know if I had ever been hit before. I told him yes, and he tried so hard to make me believe that it wasn't okay to be hit, but I didn't let it sink in. My mom used to spank me when I lived in Haiti, but I was used to it; it was part of my culture.

I told him about my dream that a guy would be following me in the streets at night; it was always dark, and I was lost. Not knowing where I was going in the dream, I always seemed to find my old house. The door was always unlocked. I always wished my mom wasn't there, because even in the dream, I knew she was dead, but she was always on the bed, and the dream was over.

I must have had that dream at least ten times a year. I told him that my mom had died and that my dad was not involved in my life.

"Who do you live with?" he asked.

"I live alone," I replied.

"But where's home for you? Where do you go when you have breaks?" he asked.

"Nowhere," I said. "I don't go anywhere. I visit friends and family."

"How do you pay for school?"

"I get financial aid and student loans."

"You should be proud of yourself; you're a winner," he said.

He asked me what I thought of the weather that morning. I told him the weather was bad.

"Why?" he asked.

"It's cloudy; there's no sun."

"I think it's a beautiful day. It's not raining, and it's not snowing," he said.

That was the day I learned of a glass half full of water and to learn to focus on the half that's full instead of the half that's empty.

I told him about how my relationship with Kurt ended because I was too negative. But the therapist tried to convince me that it was Kurt's loss. Kurt didn't deserve me because I was too good for him.

"You have good manners, and you are well-spoken," he said. He advised me to think of myself as one in a million. I walked out of that office feeling a little better. Someone had listened to me, and I didn't feel like a failure like I had before.

Wow! One in a million. People had told me before that one does not influence another's life; we're responsible for our lives and decisions. I agreed to a certain extent, based on my own experiences. After so many years of being told that I wasn't good enough and would never be anything in life, I tended to believe it and stopped trying. Although I felt like a loser at times, like I hadn't accomplished anything, I felt like I had a lot to be proud of. I also thought of my cousin Yves's words to me before I left for college after telling him that he could not live in my shoes for one day.

"I respect you," he said. "If you ever want to make it in this life, forget about everyone, care only about what makes you happy. Make believe that you're the only one living on this planet, and there's no one else to help you if you fall."

That was by far the best advice anyone had ever given me. So, I decided, although I had fallen plenty of times, those times were the empty half of the glass that I was focusing on. I needed to focus on all the times that I had gotten up right after falling; those times would represent the full half of the glass.

I went to see the shrink once a week after that, and when he retired, I started to see a female psychologist. I liked her too. She was a good listener; she seemed like she cared. I saw her at least once a week for almost a semester. She had a unique way of getting inside my mind; she always seemed to be able to make me talk. I told her about my mood swings and how angry I got at times. She suggested that I write my feelings down when I was mad and read whatever I wrote the following day, or whenever I was feeling better.

It was Thanksgiving break, and my roommate, Emma, and I made plans to cook dinner. We also invited my previous roommate, Soo-ah and her boyfriend. Emma made the salad, Soo-ah made beef patties, and I made the rice, lasagna, chicken, and macaroni salad, all Haitian-style. I could not stop myself from laughing that night when it was time for us to eat at the table.

We lived in an off-campus apartment, which was not fancy at all. None of our chairs seemed to match. It was so funny when we had to put our food on the table because the chicken was already dried. My lasagna burned, Soo-ah's patties were salty, and we could not find enough chairs and utensils for all of us. I guess I was embarrassed more than the others because I lived there; Emma, on the other hand, didn't seem to care. Even with all this embarrassment, it was one of the best times of my life.

The following day, I talked to my old friend, David, who was then attending law school in France. He always said France had the best law schools and was cheaper. David was from Haiti, and although he was much older, I seemed to like him. He appeared to be ready for something that guys my age weren't prepared for: a commitment and the desire for a family of his own. When we first met, he always told me that he was persistent when he wanted something and never gave up just because someone gave him the cold shoulder. The first time he ever said, "I love you," I was shocked. I didn't know what to say, so I told him I had to go to class. He said it until he got tired of it and never repeated it.

David started to turn cold just when I began to give him a little attention; he knew I liked him then. No calls, he was always busy, always too tired, he seemed to have been getting amnesia. I called him the day after Thanksgiving, and I wanted to talk, but he couldn't. He said he had to cook, but it seemed like he couldn't cook while he was on the phone.

"I'll call you as soon as I'm done," he said and hung up.

"He doesn't want me anymore," I said to myself. I got quiet, my heart started to beat fast, and I felt like my chest and throat were getting tight. I didn't want to cry because Emma would've asked me what was wrong, and I would've had to tell her, but I could not because I was too embarrassed. Why did I even care?

We were only friends. It's not like he was my boyfriend. Why did it bother me so much that certain people didn't care about me? I should be enough for myself.

All of a sudden, I was too tired to do anything; I was sleepy but could not fall asleep when I went to bed. I started to feel rejected and alone, as usual. Why didn't he love me anymore? I must've done something wrong for him to be so mean toward me. Soon, I stopped watching television in the living room; I stopped joking around with Emma like I usually did. Nothing seemed to be able to make me happy. None of my favorite CDs worked. I could not see the light anymore; everything was dark and ugly. I started to notice my four walls, and the place seemed empty. I wanted so much for him to love me, not because of the person he was, but because I wanted someone to love me.

I knew there had to be something special about me if another human being could love me, but if no one could stand to be next to me, I had to be a horrible person. It all came back to me at that point. Why did I need so much for a stranger to love me? Why couldn't I make myself happy? I took my shrink's advice and decided to write down everything I was feeling inside in that dark moment.

It was the only way I was going to get to the source of why I was always so empty inside. How could I deal with something that I didn't know? The idea was to read what I wrote down when I was happy; then I could see what was inside my heart when I was sad.

"How could you do this to me?
Love me and then leave me
all alone in this dangerous world.

I don't know how much longer I can hold on.
Everyone says I'm strong.
If only they knew I'm as weak as a fly,
there's nothing inside of me.
It's so empty in there.
Why doesn't anyone care?
It's not supposed to be like this.
I've done everything by the book,
followed all the rules
and still taste the bitter part of life.
Why doesn't anyone see?
There's a heavy weight squeezing my heart,
I'm almost out of breath,
 I'm dying inside,
I want to believe that it's going to be okay
but it's not getting any better.
The years end the same way they start.
Dark, empty, full of sorrow and grief.
Why did you have to die?
Couldn't you stay with me a little bit longer?
You're the only human being who ever loved me.
I need you so much in my life.
Your touch, kind words, and your shoulder to cry on.
I'm so alone, there's no one around,
just this unfair world and me.
Everything is against me.
I've strived to be happy with no success.
I'm losing strength.
I don't think I can hold on anymore.
I'm so weak,

I'm so tired,
I'm sinking.
Somebody, please help, help, help …"

Once I didn't have anything to write anymore, I felt a heavy weight lifted from my heart. That night when I got online, I realized that my childhood friend, Marjorie, had added me on her buddy list. I couldn't believe the relief that I got inside just knowing that I was going to be able to speak to someone who would understand what I was going through. I knew if there was one person on this planet who could understand every one of my feelings, it would be her.

Marjorie's parents died in a car accident when she was just a little girl, and she was raised by her grandmother. I was sure there were nights when she wished she had her mom there to hold her. I remember when I was a child, my mom would kiss my wounds whenever I fell, and the pain would always go away. She held me at night when I was sick, and when I needed some physical touch, I would put my head on her lap and she would caress it. I was sure Marjorie had the same feelings I was having, the desire to feel loved, even by a stranger.

When I told her I was depressed that night, she went straight to the point. She listed all of my emotions: tired, sleepy, not hungry, headaches, a desire to be alone, sad, lost, crying uncontrollably, feeling worthless, hopeless, agony—and she was right. She assured me that there wasn't anything wrong with the way I was feeling and that I wasn't the only one feeling that way. She even took the time to tell me things that she usually did when she became overwhelmed by those feelings.

I realized that I wasn't crazy, there wasn't anything wrong with me, and someone else had been through the same stuff. That same night I decided to go to the movies; it was Marjorie's idea. It felt good to leave the house. I blasted my portable CD player, and it was my way of blocking out the outside world. That night I watched *The Haunted Mansion*. I didn't have fun at the movies, but I realized that I felt better than the previous days.

The next day I read my so-called poem, and I realized that it was never about David or anyone else. My feelings were all related to my mom not being there, the emptiness inside my heart. Of course, no one on this earth would be able to fill it up; I only had one mom, and she was gone. The best thing was to learn to deal with not having her in my life and move on to doing the things that she would want me to do if she were alive.

The following Monday, I decided to see the doctor because my stomach was still hurting. I told her I needed some medicine to make the pain go away. Every test she performed came back negative. I didn't know what to do when she told me that there wasn't anything wrong with me. She suggested that I take things easy and rest. I sat there like a dummy with tears in my eyes. I couldn't go on for another hour with that feeling inside my stomach. She was the doctor, and it was her job to make me feel better. She referred me to my shrink; I was allowed to see her after just a few minutes. I sat there, crying for no reason. By then, I had gotten pretty comfortable with her; I felt like I could tell her anything. I told her how much I hated my life and that it was unfair that I couldn't have a regular experience like everyone else.

"Why do you feel this way?" she asked.

"I don't know," I replied.

All of a sudden, I went off the subject. I told her about how hard life was as a Haitian. *When I'm in America, I am Haitian.* People misjudged me before they got a chance to know me. And when I was in Haiti, people saw me as an American because I didn't do things that regular Haitians did. I didn't belong anywhere and wasn't entirely accepted anywhere. I explained to her that I often felt lost; I wasn't needed. I told her about all the nights that I had gone to bed crying.

"Why doesn't anyone love me?" I asked her. "Why did my mom have to die? Why do good people die, and bad ones live longer?" I always asked myself those questions, but never to someone in person. It was too embarrassing. "I need my mom," I said while sobbing in her office.

She offered me some tissues and asked about school.

"How are things in school?" she asked.

"Bad, I can't do my work," I replied.

"Do you try?"

"Yes, but I can't. My brain doesn't work."

I cried the entire time in her office while she just sat there staring at me; I guess she didn't know what to say.

"Would you like me to sign you out of school?" she asked.

"No, I don't want to lose the entire semester."

It was only a few weeks before the semester ended, but I couldn't study for exams. I had worked too hard just to lose a whole semester like that. So instead, she sent letters to my professors, asking them to accept late work from me because I wasn't feeling well. She was afraid I was having a nervous breakdown.

CHAPTER 20

CHOOSING TO BE HAPPY

After years of empty feelings and depression, I finally wanted to find answers. I thought about my siblings. I thought we lived similar lives. Weren't we all alone and striving to make it? I imagined Paul had to be feeling the same way I felt, if not worse, because he had never even seen a picture of his mother. Although Sheila and I still talked, we were not close like we'd been before. She was always ready to bite someone, and for a while, I refused to waste my time or energy on her. Eventually, though, I decided to talk to Sheila. I wanted to know if I was making up my problems; I wanted to know if it was all in my head. Maybe I was at fault. Sheila and I had grown up together, and if my heart was so empty, I didn't see how hers could be filled with love. But what if she were *okay*—what would that say about me?

At first, she was grouchy when I told her I wanted to ask her some questions, but then she agreed when I told her to go to Hell. I told her to feel free to say whatever she was feeling, no matter what it was.

"Nadia and her family destroyed my life," she said. "They wanted her kids to be above us, but Micho never saw it like that." As imperfect as Haiti was, Sheila preferred to live there. "We didn't have money, but we had love and not too many bad moments," she said.

Tears ran down my face as I wrote down the words hidden inside my sister's heart for so many years. I always thought she was happy because, unlike me, she never had to see a shrink, or better yet, never wished she were dead. I cried because she was describing my life—sad, unfulfilled. She spoke my words before I even told her. We shared more than a mother and father; we shared the same miserable experiences. I realized that we were both empty, and all those times she was ready to bite people, it was her cry for love that no one was able to see or hear.

I stayed quiet on the phone as she said, "I'm always unhappy, money or no money. Whatever they did to me, I'll carry it throughout my life. It's going to affect my future husband and future children if I don't stop it right now. It's like a scar inside my heart; it can't be erased."

It took me so long to see that my sister's soul was bleeding just like mine; I promised myself never to walk away from her again, no matter what she did to me.

"Mothers love their children, even when the fathers walk away," she said. "Even if Mom didn't have money, we always got good food on our birthdays; we always got to eat the biggest fish on our birthday. Right now, life sucks. I think of the things

I could've done, where I would've been. Maybe it's God's will, so I will not fight reality. People say I will never be anything in life," she said.

That's what we say in my culture: mothers love their children more than fathers do—although that's not always the case. There are extraordinary fathers out there who fight for their children's happiness every single day. But mine was not one of them.

I felt guilty after talking to Sheila. I felt sorry that I had stayed away from her for so long. I always saw her as an annoying young woman, who, even though she was in her twenties, acted like an old woman. I used to wonder why she didn't care about me; she seemed to care more about her friends. She never really had the time to listen to me, and she was always ready to snap at me no matter what I had to say.

She told me that people called her a stupid slut. "I am a failure, just like they said," she said. "When I picture my life as a slut, I am a good one. Although I took people's money to pay bills, no one can say they saw the color of my underwear or slept with me. I don't deny taking money from men in the past. I did it so we could make it," she said.

Like my mom, people smiled at our faces but called us bitches behind our backs.

"If only Micho loved Mom, she wouldn't have died; she would've been right here with us," Sheila continued. "We thought we were coming to paradise, but it was Hell."

That night, I realized that Sheila had been depressed all those years, just like me. My depression only showed more because I had the guts to admit it to everyone. I got into reading every book I could get my hands on about depression. I was no better than my sister, just a little stronger. All the times I had heard things about her, I never defended her. I added to her broken heart. I hated the fact that I wasn't there for her all those years. We shared the same blood, we grew in the same womb, and it was my responsibility to make sure she was okay since no one else was going to do it for either one of us.

I needed to change the way others saw her. From that day on, I decided that I was going to defend her to anyone who called her names, no matter who it was. I would never turn my back on her again; I would give her a bit of my strength. She had fallen for so long and never gotten up. I was going to give her a hand and help her get to the place we needed to be. That's what family was for, to stick around when things got dark and ugly. She was my family, and above everything else, she loved me, and I loved her. I started to remember the time we spent living in that efficiency, when she worked as a cashier in that restaurant, cleaning tables and floors to take care of both of us.

She suffered so I didn't have to; she carried the burden and weight that I was supposed to carry. She never got up after falling because she was burned out from carrying me. She carried my weight for too long, and now it was my turn to help her carry her weight. I promised her that when I graduated from college, I was going to take care of her. I was going to have her move in with me so she could go to school. She laughed as if I were kidding. She felt like she was too old to have someone else take care of her. She didn't get it, but I was serious. I was going to take care of my sister if it was the last thing I did on this earth.

We had failed my mom; we had embarrassed her; we had done the only thing she asked us not to do when we got here. We were supposed to stick together and care for each other, but we split right after her death. Instead of crying over what I wasn't doing right, I decided that I was going to look forward to the positive things that I had to get done. I would never be able to care for my mom again; I would never be able to give her a good life and travel with her all over the world. I would never build her that mansion in Haiti, but I could help my sister get her life in order. I could help her find happiness within her heart because, just like me, she'd been looking for it in all the wrong places.

I started talking to my friend, George, a counseling student at the college. We'd been friends for about three years, so I felt pretty comfortable that I could trust him. I needed to know why so many little things brought back unbearable sadness into my life. There had to be a better way of handling matters. I learned from George that it all started at home.

"It's a result of poor coping skills in the family system," he said. As he explained, I was never taught how to properly deal with certain situations, so I depended on pills to fill that big gap inside my heart.

"If someone calls us a bad name, we take it personally. We believe that everything people say is true, so we feel belittled," he said.

He was right; I did believe everything people said. I remember my friend Elena told me I was crazy, and I took it personally, although she was kidding. Because in my culture, people who suffered from mental illnesses were called "crazy." I walked away and felt so small, like I wasn't worth anything. I told myself that she was right; I was crazy. I had been taking pills all those years to make my sadness go away; only an insane person would do such a thing. Of course, that was what my sick mind made me believe at the time, but that was not true.

"You feel like you can't do anything right; it's a series of layers," George said. "It's like a backpack; every book makes it heavier until you can't carry it anymore. When we have so many mean or bad things happen to us, we feel like there's no purpose; these things will break you. People go to alcohol because they feel there's no way out, sometimes suicide," he said.

He was right again. Instead of alcohol, I had gone to pills to make my problems go away. Half the time I didn't want to die; if only there had been someone around to listen, to tell me that things were going to be alright. If only there was someone to take my burden away, even for a little while. The therapists at the mental hospital were the first ones who'd seemed to care. They'd looked at me and seen someone, a human being; they were the first ones determined to make me feel better even when they didn't know what had sent me to the hospital.

"Something's missing, people feel inadequate," George said. "It's a cycle; if they never work through what's eating at them, it keeps coming back."

Maybe that's why I felt so often like I had to die; it kept coming back because I never worked through what was eating at me. After all, I didn't know what it was. I'd never put an end to what was haunting me, so it just kept coming back, sometimes when I expected it the least.

"You sometimes feel you're not good enough because you didn't get a hundred on a test or get a raise at work," George said. "It follows you throughout your life." It had been following me. There were times I'd get a B on a test when I was expecting an A, and I did feel dumb, like I wasn't worth anything.

"Kids are degraded through emotional, mental, and physical abuse. Parents tell them, 'I wish I never had you.' Parents sometimes compare them to other children or say, 'why can't you be like John Doe's kids?'" he explained.

I can't even remember how many times I was told to be like Esther, who became my dad's stepdaughter after my dad married Nadia. She was the good apple of Micho's new family. I can't remember how many times I was called a hypocrite, told that I wasn't good enough and that he should've left me in Haiti. Maybe George was right; it was emotional and mental. Nothing I did was ever good enough. I always had to try harder to do better, but no matter what I did, it was always less than what was acceptable. And so, I was beaten as a child. I was told that it was a way of punishment.

"You will thank me one day," my parents always said. I thought of all those years that I had seen myself as lower than a dead dog in the street. I thought of all the relationships I went through. Some of them could have worked, but there was a wall inside my heart. No one could get around it, and so the relationships failed.

I got a phone call from Diana one night. Micho had been in the hospital, so I decided to give him a call. Diana was still living in Salem at the time, which is where Micho was still living. I'm not even sure how she found out, but word usually got around pretty quickly in the Haitian community.

"Alo, Papa, it's me," I said.

"Oh, my daughter, I'm sick," he said. "I'm not good at all. If I didn't come here last night, I would've died."

"What happened?"

"Too much stress."

So we talked about my siblings. They had abandoned him, so he said.

"Maybe you should ask them why," I suggested. He said he would not, that he hadn't done anything wrong to them, that it was their duty to call; his job was done. I never knew parenting was an eighteen-year job. I always thought it was a lifetime commitment made out of love.

"You're the only one who hasn't erased me from your book. You call me even when I don't call you," he said to me.

I finally had the courage to tell my father how much he had hurt me. I told him about my emptiness, the depression, the sadness. I told him how his absence affected me throughout the years. I told him how he'd been complicit in allowing others to hurt his children while giving his love to another man's children. I told him how the way he treated my mom had affected me as a woman. He didn't even show up to her funeral. I told him we all stayed away because we couldn't handle the pain he caused. Because of his absence, I had looked for love in all the wrong places and had gotten hurt too many times. I had dealt with homelessness, and nearly died in an abusive relationship. All before I was twenty-one years old.

I told him he was not a good father. He had refused to sign my financial aid application so I could get out of poverty. He'd walked away from us and didn't look back. I expected him to hang up on me, but he didn't. He listened and said, "Okay."

He surprised me. Haitian children were not supposed to speak to their parents in that tone. They were supposed to remain quiet when their parents talked, even when the parents were wrong. In a sense, they were expected to remain children even when they became adults themselves. Maybe this was a sign that Micho was changing. Maybe staying away from him for a few years made him realize that it was possible to lose us forever, because even after everything he had done, he still thought he loved us and did the best for us. Maybe I could still salvage my relationship with my dad.

As angry as I was, I still needed him and I still loved him. I needed to heal, and I could not heal without making amends with those who had hurt me.

"I'm graduating soon," I told him. He asked for the date. "December 17th," I told him.

"As long as we're both alive, I'll be there," he said. "I'm going to clap until my arms fall off," he added, so I laughed. "I'm going to be proud of myself; I'm going to be proud of you," he said.

Happy tears came to my eyes. I had waited over ten years to hear him say something like that, and it was probably the nicest thing he'd ever said to me. Finally, he'd found interest in knowing what I was studying.

"I hope you get a good job," he said.

I wanted him to come; I wanted him to see me in my cap and gown. I wanted him to know that even without his help, I got to wear that gown.

That conversation was the turning point in my relationship with my dad. I earned his respect that day, and he never disrespected me again. After that conversation, I became the good daughter; I was no longer a hypocrite like he thought before. I was the one who called and visited everyone, even when none of those favors were returned.

I was also the one who cried herself to sleep almost every night because my phone didn't ring. I'm not sure if I should call it a relationship, for it was a one-way street. I tried so hard to be part of such relationships. Why did I need so much for my dad to be in my life? There were times when I made myself believe that he loved me, and maybe he did in his own way. The incident that kept me going was when I was maybe four years old—he would always place me on his feet and dance with me. I couldn't seem to get that picture out of my head. Only a loving father would dance with his toddler and hold her hand to teach her how to write. Only a loving father would pay his child's tuition. Only a loving father would pay the rent and provide food for his child.

The more I talked to Micho and reached out to others, the better I felt. I was becoming a better person; I was happier. The more I forgave, the freer I became. I realized that the world had something to offer; I could get married, have kids, or maybe adopt. I decided to remove the wall that I'd placed around my heart so I could love and forgive others. I decided to go back to church; God had always been the one Father to me who never stopped doing His job.

I realized that I had a lot to be thankful for. I ate every day, had a roof over my head, and had breath inside of me. I stopped looking at the empty half of the glass and focused on the half that was full. I decided to count my blessings and not my sorrows. I chose to cherish my friends and my family, especially the younger ones. I decided to be a better listener and care more about others when they needed help, for I knew what it felt like to need someone to care.

I started talking to Paul again. By then, he had married Guerda and had a baby girl, Marissa. My brother's presence in my life was the icing on the cake. A couple weeks before graduation, I took a bus ride to Salem for Thanksgiving break. I stayed with Diana. I finally had the courage to visit my brother and Guerda's place. When I walked into their apartment that day, I saw Guerda sitting on a sofa with Marissa on her lap. She looked beautiful. Marissa stared at me as if she had seen me before. I asked if I could hold her.

"Of course you can," Guerda replied. Holding my niece for the first time was one of my most enjoyable experiences. I was an auntie. Guerda made it clear to me the baby had nothing to do with whatever had happened between us in the past. I appreciated that, because regardless of how I felt about her, I loved her child. Loving her child meant I needed to love her too and accept her as my sister-in-law.

After years of wishing, my phone finally started ringing regularly. It was usually Paul calling to check on me and to apologize. Micho started checking on me too. He stopped complaining for the most part.

Micho changed his mind about coming to my college graduation. I didn't ask why. I didn't really care. I had already made it this far without him. Paul and Sheila could not make it either. Most of my family and friends could not come, except for Martin, and my cousin Steven, who lived in Canada at the time.

Paul took me to a car auction in New Jersey during Thanksgiving break. There, I purchased an old white Chevy for exactly $1,000. I worked at the college front desk during my last semester, so I was able to save some money. I needed the car to move my stuff from the off-campus house to a new place in Salem, where I had rented a room from a Haitian couple. The plan was to leave the car at the auction until I could register it in Massachusetts. Paul promised to go back to New Jersey and pick up my car in time for graduation and then drive me back to Salem. This was before he decided he could no longer come to the graduation.

After asking several friends and family members for help to no avail, Paul agreed to drive me to New Jersey to pick up my car, but I would have to drive myself back to Salem. This was good enough for me. I reached Salem late Thursday night and stayed with Diana. The next day, Paul and I left for New Jersey.

Everything was going as planned. We went to the auction, showed the paperwork, screwed the license plates on the car, and we hit the road. Since Paul had been to that auction before, we agreed that I would follow him closely. As we drove on the interstate, Paul started switching lanes frequently. I didn't have a GPS with me, so it was imperative that I follow him until we reached our destination.

It started to get dark, and all of a sudden, it started raining. I didn't have a cellphone, so I couldn't call Paul to tell him to slow down, and in the blink of an eye, his car disappeared. I was lost. I drove until I ran out of gas. It was close to 11 p.m. when Kurt called to ask if I was excited about graduation. I had pulled over for coffee somewhere in Connecticut. I was crying. Kurt wanted me to drive to the nearest airport so he could fly me to Massachusetts. He wanted me to walk in my graduation.

"I can't," I said. "I need to move my stuff out of my apartment by Sunday because I need my deposit back." How I reached Salem is still a blur. Although I asked a few people directions, it always seemed like I had a guardian angel guiding me. I reached Diana's house in the middle of the night. It must have been 2 in the morning when I went to bed and promised myself I would wake up before dawn to drive to North Adams in time for graduation, which was taking place at 10 a.m. that morning.

Early that morning, I called Elena to let her know I was on my way. "It's snowing heavy," she said. At that point, I realized that there was no way I could make it in time for graduation. By the time I made it to North Adams, both Martin and Steven were gone. The graduation was over.

Seeing my friends' graduation pictures was bittersweet. Elena even got a graduation champagne glass for me at our graduation party. The date was December 17, 2005. I was jealous. I deserved to walk across that stage. I worked hard for that day. I earned it. I was tired of losing. When would my winning day come? Would it ever come? I decided the diploma would have to suffice. I had to move forward with my life. This was just one more bump I had to overcome on my way to success.

I used my deposit refund to rent a room from a Haitian couple Rachelle referred me to. They rented me the room for $350 as a favor to Rachelle.

A couple of weeks after graduation, Johnny and I got into a huge argument over Elena. He had sent her an email, telling her that I was crazy. How could Johnny betray me like this? He was my best friend. I trusted him with my life. I confronted him, and he apologized. I felt betrayed. I loved this person with every fiber of my being. I loved him enough to give him a kidney if he ever needed one.

Once again, my low self-esteem would not allow me to overlook what he had done. I could not forgive him. However, all Johnny wanted was for me to forgive him and move on as friends, but I could not. He had hurt me. How could I ever trust him? I was filled with emotions.

"Are you going to forgive me or not?" he asked.

"No," I replied. "I don't think we should be friends anymore." I hung up the phone and blocked Johnny's number. I refused to be disrespected. Those days were over. I lost my best friend.

I sat in my empty room with the futon Rachelle had given me and a table I picked up from the trash. I was angry. My head started hurting, and I began to cry. Would this ever end? My stomach started hurting. The pain was excruciating. I was tired. I put some orange juice in a glass with a few aspirins until they dissolved. I needed this pain to go away. I sat at the table, staring at the glass for over an hour. I cried and stared. Eventually, I got up, picked up the glass, and walked toward the restroom. I flushed the juice and aspirins. That was the last time I ever felt like I needed to harm myself. It was also the beginning of my new life. A very beautiful one.

EPILOGUE

Three years after graduating college, I met a wonderful guy named Hunter. We were inseparable almost immediately. By then, I had already relocated to South Carolina for work. We spent a big chunk of our time going to the beach, eating out, and visiting theme parks. We took many short weekend getaways together. I went back to school and got my Master's in Business Administration. By then, I had already been working for a major company in the United States, making a decent wage. The company paid for most of the tuition. I had crawled my way out of poverty.

My dad and I became very close over time. We spoke often, and he knew he could count on me for anything. I talked to his doctors for him as needed. I drove him around when I was in Salem, and I gave him money when needed. He called when he didn't hear from me, and he stopped complaining. He no longer allowed others to trash me behind my back. He was proud of me and made it known to everyone. My siblings and I reconnected. We checked on each other every now and then. Sheila and I talked at least once a month; Paul and I talked more often. I never talked to Nadia again. As much as I wanted to make peace and forgive others so I could heal, I also needed to keep negativity out of my life. I no longer allowed toxicity around me.

Hunter and I got married one year after we met. I looked like a princess that day. My dad walked me down the aisle and gave me away, which was mostly symbolic. Diana was my maid of honor. My goddaughter, Sonya, was my junior bridesmaid.

My dad liked Hunter. My wedding day was bittersweet. I felt my mother's absence in the days before the wedding and even more during that day. I shed a few tears here and there, but I had to accept the fact that I couldn't change what was. I lit a candle in her memory. My roommates, Isaiah and Emma, were guests at the wedding. Emma helped me get dressed. As much as I wished my mom could have done it, I felt blessed to have had such great friends in my life to fill those shoes. I was also glad to have had Martin at my wedding. He was like a second dad to me.

A few years after our wedding, Hunter and I had a beautiful baby girl named Thea—meaning "blessings of the Lord." I had received so many blessings from God over the years, but Thea was the best one. She became the apple of my eye and my purpose for living. Her eyes were hazel just like her dad's.

My dad died in his sleep not long after Thea was born. Hunter and I paid for his funeral. His funeral depicted that of a man who had worked hard and was sent off with high honors.

Life has been good to me. Every now and then, depression sneaks up on me, but I know that life is worth every breath I get to take on this earth. I know that tomorrow can get better. All I have to do is press pause and wait for the storm to pass. I know that I don't need anyone or anything to make me whole. My happiness comes from within me, and I am enough.

REFLECTION

When I look in the mirror, I still see a reflection of you.

Sometimes I even think I see you—
that time you tickled me on the ground under the coconut tree
in our backyard.

I can still smell the Vicks you rubbed on my chest
that night I had bronchitis,
taste that teardrop from your eye
the day that rock broke my head,
feel your arms tight around me when I was sad.

My soul is starving for your love,
my dreams are filled with the wrinkles on your face
when you smiled.

If only I'd had the chance to say goodbye …

Tears alone would explain the unsaid words.

I live your life as if you are melted into me.

I'm changed forever—
no happiness to ever overcome that sadness
like an ocean without water.

My one special date in a year becomes my worst:

We were one that day, now apart.

Just one last time, I want to wrap my arms around you
as you did for me,
and whisper in your ears those words
that went untold.

Maybe you already knew
you loved me just as much and more.

At least I make myself believe that
so I can keep going
and be that person you raised me to be:

A reflection of you.

ABOUT THE AUTHOR

Jeanne is the author of *Mommy, I Need My Wheels*, a children's book about a little boy who is learning to ride a bike without training wheels, and *Out of the Darkness*, a Young Adult novel about the life of an immigrant teenager from Haiti. Her latest book is *Suzette and the One-Eyed Cat*, a story about a little girl adopted from Haiti who meets her biological family for the first time.

Today, fueled by a desire to inspire children, young adults, and women, she writes authoritatively and creatively on issues of social justice to help others cope with life's predicaments.

Born and raised in Haiti, Jeanne currently lives in the United States with her husband and children. She enjoys watching TV, reading, and traveling the world. She is the founder of *Learn Haitian Creole / Aprann Kreyòl Ayisyen*, a website that provides texts, games, and videos for those interested in learning Haitian Creole.

www.jeannefortune.com